SHOW
ME THE
MONEY

SHOW ME THE MONEY

ELAMITA

Srishti
Publishers & Distributors

Srishti Publishers & Distributors
Registered Office: N-16, C.R. Park
New Delhi – 110 019
Corporate Office: 212A, Peacock Lane
Shahpur Jat, New Delhi – 110 049
editorial@srishtipublishers.com

First published by
Srishti Publishers & Distributors in 2019

10 9 8 7 6 5 4 3 2 1

This is a work of fiction. The characters, places, organisations and events described in this book are either a work of the author's imagination or have been used fictitiously. Any resemblance to people, living or dead, places, events, communities or organisations is purely coincidental.

Printed and bound in India

To my deity.
To my family.
To myself.

Push yourself, because no one is going to do it for you.

Acknowledgements

It gives me immense pleasure that my book *Show Me the Money* is being published by Srishti Publishers.

The journey of writing this book has been nothing less than a roller coaster ride for me. The idea of writing was seeded back in 2014, but it took me almost five years to get the book in my hands. In fact, my baby and this book have grown up simultaneously. It took lots of exploration, research and analysis before putting the facts into the form of a story.

Devastated by the news of tampering in cricket matches gave birth to the author in me and led me to discover a platform where one can speak straight from the soul.

Prologue

It was raining outside. I reached the edge of the window and inhaled the delightful petrichor. I closed my eyes in a blend of happy satisfaction; it was the aroma of my land, of my country.

Rain in Delhi, in November, was unusual; but I loved it. I put my hand out of the window and felt it. The tenderness in the raindrops not only wet my hand, but also my heart. Mesmerisingly, I gazed at flowers and plants, nodding in the rain with joy; a couple of pigeons were splashing water on each other. A five-years-old boy came out to play in the garden with his puppy. I loved watching them.

But somewhere inside, I felt sick. I felt a strange emptiness deep inside my heart. This misery was associated with the demise of my dearest pal, Gourav. Just a few days ago, I heard Richa calling me, her voice clear and loud as she entered the room. "Amit… Amit… the news on the television…" I turned towards her, wondering what was so important that she had come running, and almost screaming. She was panting. "Police has arrested some bookie named Naseef Ali; he has revealed the name behind Gourav's murder," she said.

I rushed to watch the news, joining mom and dad.

The news reader kept talking sophisticatedly, "*Naseef Ali, a bookmaker, had been holed up in Multan, Pakistan, for the last two months. Yesterday, he was caught by the Punjab police in Patiala at a five-star hotel. The arrest assumes importance as the police believes he could divulge the names of those involved in cricket match-fixing scandals.*

He has also disclosed information about the slaying of Gourav Mishra, a businessman and bookmaker who was killed last month by an unknown assailant. Gourav Mishra was a key vouchee for the police in the latest cricket match-fixing scandals. He'd also helped police in raiding several illegal bookmaking centres.

As per Naseef Ali's claims, Pushkar Mehta, the head syndicate in bookmaking, is the man behind Gourav Mishra's killing.

Naseef confessed during an interrogation that he had suffered a lot due to Gourav Mishra, and always wanted vengeance. He had talked to Pushkar Mehta and found that the latter was also displeased with Gourav Mishra's double-dealing and turning hostile on them. Pushkar is then reported to have ordered his minions to finish Gourav off."

In one corner of the screen, the news channel was flashing pictures of Naseef Ali, Pushkar Mehta and Gourav on loop.

"It is not easy to arrest Pushkar Mehta; these people grow under the wing of the underworld, gangsters and get protection from them. Although the police have issued an arrest warrant against him, still he's roaming freely. Our police and the whole system is paralysed in front of these criminals," I muttered disappointedly.

Richa gave me a concerned look and rubbed my shoulder gently. She could discern my mental state very well. In losing a friend so dear to me, I had felt a huge loss which could never be recovered. Only time could help blanket the grief and some real breaking news bubbling with the confirmation of 'the end' of Pushkar Mehta and his companions.

The very next day, I was leaving for Germany with my wife. Our vacation in India was over. After spending one month in Delhi, now it was finally time to go back to work. Now, it was time to move far from my roots, once again.

I started packing my bags. I picked up an album of my college days and put it inside my bag. I wanted to take those wonderful memories along with me – memories of those fun days, memories of friends, memories of family… and memories of Gourav, my dearest buddy.

PART I

I and my wife Richa had been in Germany for the last three years. My family was in Delhi. When you're abroad, you miss your family and pals like a four-year-old kid who misses his mom at school.

So this year, we planned a vacation to India, in time to enjoy Dussehra and Diwali with my folks. Mom had told me so many times that these festivals had been less alluring for them as Richa and I were not there. Diwali in our family is opulent: throughout the week, we visit our relatives, exchange gifts and sweets, play cards and make merry. In Germany, I missed all these moments; that's why I planned the vacation at a time when we could celebrate the festivals as well.

A day before leaving for India, I sat down to call up my friends. I wanted to tell them I'd be there for a month, and we should catch up as much as possible. Gourav's mobile was switched off. Next, I called up Nitin. To my dismay, he told me someone had stabbed Gourav a night before; Nitin himself was at the hospital at that time.

"How is he? What are the doctors saying?" I asked impatiently, holding my breath.

"He has major injuries; doctor says he got stabbed thrice. His intestines and one of his kidneys are badly damaged.

He has lost a lot of blood. He is very critical, Amit," Nitin lamented.

Moments before, euphoria was waving inside me. I was chuckling with the thoughts of banter with my chums. I was confused whether this packing would ever end as there were enough Diwali gifts for every single person. Mom's special dishes were mouth-watering even in my imagination. But that one phone call had left me dumbstruck.

"When is your flight?" Nitin asked me, to break the silence.

"Tomorrow morning at 5:30," I mumbled.

"Come soon … I'm missing you… Rajeev is also reaching here tomorrow morning. I wish we four could reunite!"

"We will Nitin, sure thing. Nothing would go wrong, have faith. Be with his family until we reach. Uncle and aunty must be shattered … How is Shalini?"

"She is in the hospital all the time, trying to be strong enough to give emotional support to his parents," Nitin said.

Back to India

We boarded the flight, and after takeoff, the air hostesses got occupied with making passengers comfortable; serving snacks and drinks. My gaze was somewhere outside the window. We were passing through a castle of clouds, the bright white cotton buds spread all over the sky. My eyes were pinned outside, but my mind was rewinding the pages of my life. I was devastated after hearing about Gourav.

Gourav was my dearest friend. Together we had spent the best ever days in our college. He was polite, emotional and vulnerable, but full of life. He was always a friend in need. Where was I when he was in trouble? My heart ached at the thought.

I remembered the incident from back then, at the height of a thousand feet above sea level, when I found myself dangling in the air. I could see bushes and trees spread below me, and on some distance, I could get the view of the river Ganga also. My hands and legs were free and swinging in the air. I was almost flying in air, but something had clutched on to my haunches and stopped me from falling. Or, probably my jacket was hooked in one of the branches of a tree. Everything happened so quickly that I couldn't make sense out of it.

It was Dehradun and I had come with my college group for camping. We had to start trekking, but a downpour had ruined the entire plan. After it stopped, I decided to go out and capture the beautiful scenery in my camera, since I loved photography. Gourav joined me as well.

We reached a hill, from where the view was awesome. A huge rainbow had bloomed out after the rain in the valley, and behind the rainbow was an enormous amount of water hailing down with e'lan from the cliff of mountain. The valley was looking mesmerisingly youthful. I proceeded towards the cliff to take some wonderful shots. But, Mother Nature had some other plans. Suddenly, my shoes slipped on the muddy grasses, I lost my balance and ended up dangling on a tree, almost like a bat.

I could hear Gourav's panicked voice from behind, "Amit… Amit… are you all right? Can you hear me? Amit…"

"Gourav, I am down here…" I yelled. In that situation, he was my only hope.

"Hey buddy, nice position to get a better shot. How do these ideas even come to you?" I saw him coming. His edgy gesture set to tranquil seeing me hanging safely there. "How do you manage getting into unique positions every time! But it's a risk I tell you…" Gourav was carefully coming towards me. He was holding bushes and leaves with both his hands and placing his foot firmly on the rocky surface to prevent slippage.

"Stop your nonsense! It's scaring the shit out of me. Help me out here," I yelled.

Gourav tried to reach me, but in vain. "Amit, you are out of my reach. I will do one thing. I will quickly go back and call for some help. Till then, don't let go."

"Gourav, don't leave me alone. I am very scared. I don't know for how long can this branch bear my weight," I almost cried; my agitation worn on me.

"Hey! Don't even dare think of falling. I will be back soon. I saw some cranes at work beside the main road. I need to talk to them. Don't worry, you will be rescued." His words gave me some comfort and hope. Crane could be the best option for rescuing me from there. "And you know, you really can take some marvellous shots; it's a great view. You also have your camera hanging in your neck. Why don't you click…?"

"Shut up!"

Almost after ten minutes, I saw the giant yellow machine approaching me. I found composure seeing the appearance of five-six people along with Gourav. And finally, I got rescued.

We were a group of four friends in college – Gourav, Rajeev, Nitin and I. After our graduation, we all got admission for an MBA course in the same institute.

I still remember our fourth day at the institute. Ragging was the wellspring of entertainment for some of the senior students. We went to the canteen and were seized by some rude seniors.

The first lesson of management – it would not be in favour of any fresher to disobey their senior's order. Thus, we hesitantly did whatever they were asking us to do, like acting, dancing, catwalk, answering their absurd questions.

In the meantime, a girl of average height, blunt hair cut entered the canteen. She wore a light orange top with a deep orange scarf, paired with black trousers and high- heeled shoes. Wine-coloured goggles were sophisticatedly tucked on her head and adding on her stunning personality. She put her handbag on a table and pulled out a chair to sit. Then, she delicately took out some paper from her bag and began to read.

One of the seniors told Rajeev and me to serve cold drinks and samosas to her. Next, they gave a red rose to Gourav and told him to ask her out on a date. It was awkward for us, but we had no choice.

Rajeev went to her table and placed the cold drink. By the time she looked up, Rajeev had nimbly come back. With some hesitation, I held the plate of samosas and kept that on her table. This time she said, "Hey, I didn't even order yet!" But I ignored her and came back nimble-footed. After that, Gourav went, hiding the rose behind him. Perhaps he planned to present the rose after impressing her, like a cherry on a cake, just before asking her for a date.

"Hi, I'm Gourav. MBA first year," Gourav grinned. "May I?" Before she could say anything, he pulled out the chair and sat. "Well, are you also a fresher?"

She didn't reply and annoyingly, put her papers on the table.

"Managerial… Economics," Gourav read from the papers. "Hmm… so you are preparing in advance for the first class of Economics. Don't worry, people say Economics is a boring subject, but I'm good in it. I can help you. These graphs and curves are not rocket science, I tell you. It's the boring faculty that make this subject boring… like them! Otherwise, it's a very interesting subject!"

She looked at him and smiled, "Nice to hear that you find it interesting."

Gourav looked at us out of the corners of his eyes; the whole group was watching him. He got a bit more confident to go ahead when she smiled. "Your smile is perfect. If you don't mind, may I tell you something?" Now her smile vanished and she looked at Gourav, suspiciously. "Your eyes are very pretty. Your smile directly connects to your eyes. I am surprised I'm saying these lines to someone in our very first meet!"I think he was parroting romantic lines from a novel or movie.

And when he was done, he held out the red rose and said, "Will you be my friend, or shall I say, a special friend? I'll be glad if you accept this."

She looked around; all the students were watching them. She grumbled, "What nonsense is going on here?" and sprang up from the chair. I looked at the seniors; they were smirking. She, in a fit of pique, collected her papers, put them inside her handbag, and scowled, "It's too much. The guts of this student, flirting with a teacher! I am your faculty, boy. Kiran Rao, who will teach you theories of Economics, so stay within your limits, and learn some respect." With that, she left.

Gourav was shocked and embarrassed. The other students were laughing and mocking him. We left the canteen as soon as possible. We had the Managerial Economics class next, but Gourav didn't attend it. He was feeling sheepish. He broke out in a cold sweat whenever Kiran Rao was in front of him. The entire semester, either he bunked her classes, or he used to sit far at the back where he couldn't be seen by her.

❖

"What would you like to have, sir?" The sweet voice of an air hostess interrupted my thoughts.

"Aaah, just a cup of coffee," I said.

She gently poured coffee into the cup and asked again, "Anything else, sir?"

"No thanks."

With a sip of coffee, I slipped back to the memory lane.

By the end of the last semester, we four had jobs in hand. At campus placement, I was selected by a telecom company. Nitin and Rajeev together were selected by a banking company and Gourav was selected by a pharmaceuticals company.

That was the happiest moment of our life. We felt like conquering the world.

Gourav was posted to Jaipur, Nitin to Gurgaon and Rajeev to Noida. My posting was in Chennai.

Life without buddies

The cabin lights of the flight were dimmed to make passengers comfortable to slip into a slumber. Richa had slept by then, her head resting on my shoulder.

I rested mine against hers and thought, 'The time I fell in love, Gourav was the first person with whom I shared my feelings for Richa. My first love would have remained in my heart itself if he hadn't helped me knocked them into shape.'

Buddies are like blessings in life. I could not imagine my life without Gourav, Nitin and Rajeev. They understood me better than me. Our bonding was such that without saying anything, we could read each other's minds. Gourav had sensed, even before me, that I was carrying soft feelings for Richa.

It'd been five years since I met her. She had come as an intern in my company, in Chennai. She was working over the project of customer behaviour; how to retain high end customers.

Our organisation was facing a sudden drop in ARPU (Average Revenue Per unit) for the last few months, then. Among several customers, two major corporate clients had withdrawn services from us. Mr Kumaram, the regional head, had formed a team of four members under my supervision to look at the matter; Richa was a part of the team.

Gourav was coming to Chennai for a couple of weeks. His train was arriving at 4:45 a.m. I knew he was not familiar with the city as it was his first time in Chennai. So, I was supposed to pick him up from the station. "You don't need to go through a brainstorming session early in the morning, I'll be there before your train reaches," I told Gourav. Though he was asking for my address, but I did not think it was necessary. I'd be there anyway.

I set an alarm of 3:30 am, and slept. I was very happy, my buddy was coming, and we had lots of things to talk about. I thought about the old days when we used to sit on the roof under the moonlit sky, quenching our throats with chilled beer along with old melodious Hindi songs, making the atmosphere perfect for the evening. There was a small shop of snacks on the roadside and the shopkeeper used to make some mouth-watering spicy snacks on our request. We four shared everything with each other.

Don't know when I dozed off, thinking about the past days. I heard some voices in my slumber. Gradually it was becoming louder… I tried to open my eyes and squinted due to a gleam from the window glass. Someone was calling my name, Amit… Amit, and banging the door. I looked at the clock cross-eyed; it was 7:40 a.m. I sprang up from the bed. I had to pick up Gourav from the station at 4:30 a.m. The alarm didn't work, damn! I opened the door. Gourav was standing in front of me. Awkwardly, I went close to him for a hug, but he pushed me back. He looked angry. "I'm sorry. I didn't reach on time," I said.

"Didn't reach on time…?" He repeated my words sarcastically. "You didn't even get up from your bed. You know what the time is?"

I looked at the clock again and wondered, "How did you reach here? Did you have my address?"

"I'm your buddy; I know you better. I was expecting this. I took the address from your dad before leaving." He chuckled and we both laughed.

In the afternoon, Gourav was watching some pictures of Pongal on my laptop which was celebrated recently in my office. Meantime, I was making tea in the kitchen, when he asked aloud, "Who is this lady?" I didn't know which picture he was looking at, but I spoke up my mind abruptly, "She is Richa!"

Gourav had caught me on my instant reply. These buddy kind of friends sometimes happen to be mischievous and naughty. He sensed out my interest in Richa. Quickly, he prepared a plot to make me confess my feelings.

I came out with a tray of tea and a plate of samosas.

"This lady, Richa, has manly features, isn't it?" He left me confused. Richa, manly features! I didn't get him. "Her big round eyes behind the specs remind me of Surendra Tripathi, our marketing professor, isn't it?"

Who the hell was Gourav talking about? I tried to look at the picture he was looking at. "Richa's hair is also similar to Tripathi sir's, greasy and jet black," Gourav said. His words drove me crazy. None of the features Gourav was describing matched Richa's personality. She was beauty; every bachelor in my office had a secret crush on her! I was sure Gourav was talking about someone else, but not Richa.

I saw the picture, it was Ms Shobha, the senior HR executive, one of the most serious and strict persons, who hardly smiled. "How could you call her Richa," I almost yelled.

"You said it!" Gourav said innocently.

I searched for a picture where Richa had posed with the *rangoli*, "Look, she is, Richa!" I said with a kind of pride in my voice. I was expecting good comments from Gourav. But, he ignored my interest mercilessly and insisted to show him the previous picture of Ms Shobha, who looked familiar to professor Tripathi! He was irritating me deliberately. Annoyingly I said, "Seeing your interest, I advise you to take transfer in Chennai. Why only Tripathi sir, you'll also get ladies resembling Chaman sir, Bhatti sir, Surender sir or, Chokhani sir!"

Gourav burst into laughter. "I love this city, interesting place. Aah!" Then, gradually he caught his breath and said, "Kick aside my interests. Let me discover yours. So, finally you are in love."

"What?" My annoyed gesture turned into clueless bombshell, "Love?"

"Pretty! And sweet also. Good choice!"

"Oh! She is not my girlfriend. She is doing her internship with our company. Helping me in a project. But, you just called her pretty and sweet. In fact, you never saw her photos properly." My gesture was more composed by then.

He grinned, took a big bite of the samosa and said stuff full-mouthed, "What do you think, were my eyes on Ms Shobha? The instant reply from the kitchen was enough to understand the love interest of my buddy."

"Love interest? Sounds good! Didn't think about yet." I sipped my tea thoughtfully.

"Oh, really!" He took another bite with the previous one still not completely swallowed, and continued, "What's the delay? And now I'm here, let me meet her too."

I sipped my tea and thought over whatever Gourav had said.

I planned for a movie with my team on Saturday. Gourav was also with me, excited to meet Richa. I introduced him to everyone. After shaking hands with Manjunath and Varun, Gourav shook hands with Richa.

She was wearing a light blue top with black jeans. She had made a high pony tail and put big round earrings on. Her bright eyes were nicely outlined with blue eyeliner, and lips with my favourite light pink lip gloss.

"Didn't know Amit's office could also have pretty faces! Aren't you from north?" Gourav asked next.

"Yeah, from Chandigarh," she replied.

"Yeah, that's what I was expecting! You don't seem to belong here."

Varun and Manjunath glared at Gourav from the corner of their eyes and looked at each other. Wasn't he speaking too much?

"Pretty, you are! And this blue colour makes you look prettier!" Gourav went on.

"Oh! Really? Thank you," Richa said gladly.

"Yeah, I am amazed, no one has told you yet? What kind of people are you working with? Praise misers!" Gourav said satirically.

I was jealous. And it was too much when he called us 'praise misers'. But he was right, everyone in office had a secret crush on Richa, but no one ever dared flirting with her. Manjunath gestured me to come in a corner with him. "Your friend is a big flirt, I tell you. What does he want to prove in front of Richa? Are we dumb and he is very cool?" he said in his Tamil accent.

I defended Gourav. I knew he was doing that purposely.

We had gone out for the latest James Bond movie. Richa sat in the corner. Gourav managed to occupy the seat just beside hers. Manjunath and Varun gave a weird look to Gourav and sat beside me. I was sitting in the middle. I elbowed Gourav hard for his act. "What are you doing?" I whispered.

"Relax… I am just making her comfortable."

"Comfortable… for what?" I asked.

"Girls love admiration; you should make her feel special. Keeping feelings for her in your heart doesn't work. You have to tell her, otherwise…"

"Otherwise… what?"

"Otherwise, some third person like me will come in between her and you," Gourav said and took the popcorn box to offer Richa. After a moment he turned to me, "Are you dying to sit here?" he asked. I didn't say anything. I pretended as I was engrossed in the movie. He whispered in my ear, "Are you interested in just watching the movie or watching the movie with your girlfriend?" I glared him back, and thought it better to exchange our seats.

Gourav had always been too involved in my life. Undoubtedly, he gets all the credit for the beginning of our love story. He was the one, who told Richa about my feelings for her, when she misunderstood that I was politically taking full credit of her hard work. Devastated, she wanted to leave Chennai and go back to Chandigarh. In the meantime, Gourav came forward as a saviour and all her misunderstandings evaporated. And the florescence of romance brought commitment in our relationship.

Every Jack has his Jill

I had accepted a job offer from a well-known German MNC and had settled there. Richa and my relationship had been revealed to both sides of the family and was accepted happily.

I used to call Richa off and on and tell her every new thing.

She had also been transferred to the Delhi office; there she was staying with her cousin, Neha. Now she could meet my friends and family often.

Gourav switched jobs and joined his new company in Delhi.

The next boy who was swept off his feet was Nitin. He fell in love with Richa's cousin Neha. Along with Richa, Neha was also involved with my friends and my family. One day, Richa told me that Neha, Nitin, Gourav, Rajeev and she had gone to watch an India v/s Australia cricket match at the Firoz Shah Kotla Stadium, Delhi. My group was dyed-in-the-wool cricket buff wherever fun betting was involved. That was the time everyone's face lit up with an impish glee. Gourav bet that Australia would score above three hundred runs. Rajeev and Neha seconded him, whereas Richa and Nitin bet on the contrary. That day, Australia scored two hundred and ninety-two runs against India. With the margin of eight to nine runs, Nitin and Richa won the bet. Gourav took all of them to Khan Market for a feast.

All that made me nostalgic. I told Richa how in our college days, we four would often bet while watching cricket. Sometimes the losing party had to treat the rest; sometimes they had to do some daring task assigned to him; and sometimes we just bet our pocket money.

I was happy indeed that everyone had been reunited at one place and they were having fun together. But, I missed them.

In March, I was coming to India for a month. On hearing this, my family had announced my engagement. Richa's parents were delighted. With everyone's consent, we got engaged on March 10th, and the wedding quickly followed on the 17th.

When I reached India, a grand welcome awaited me. This time, Richa's family was also there to welcome their future son-in-law. Richa was standing apart, smiling. She looked prettier than ever. Our families were excited about the engagement ceremony; they were busy planning everything. I could sense happiness in the air. Nitin, Gourav and Rajeev gave me a tight hug as I was the first among them to get hitched.

There was a cricket match between India and Sri Lanka on the next day. Nitin had invited us to his home to watch it. Richa and Neha were also coming to watch the match.

I was seeing Neha after a long time. Rather, I could say that it was the first time I noticed that she was beautiful. Why I hadn't noticed before, I wondered! Maybe because when you truly love someone, you stop noticing the world around you. "When are you guys getting engaged?" I asked.

"We haven't talked to our families about our relationship yet. They don't know about us."

"Come on, tell them! Don't be late in doing this. Let them know today only, both of you!" I exclaimed.

"Today? Have you gone nuts?" Nitin exclaimed. "We will talk to them for sure, but we are waiting for the right time. Neha's mother is coming to Delhi next week. She will talk to her and then I will too."

The match started, Sri Lanka was batting first. We were all engrossed. The girls brought some cold drinks and snacks. I was experiencing the high moment after a long time. At the end of the first innings, Sri Lanka had scored 312 runs after losing 5 wickets. We were discussing the game and the players.

"It's difficult for India to chase this target. Indian cricketers aren't in good form since the last three or four matches," Rajeev said.

"Yup, it seems tough. Sachin has injured his left shoulder and Virender is out of form these days," Nitin seconded Rajeev's statement.

Come on, 313 is not a huge target, and India has chased the score so many times, India will win… just watch guys, it's going to be an interesting game," Gourav countered.

And the match started. After five overs, India lost Sachin's wicket. "Ohhhh nooo," everyone screamed.

"India won't win… it is a tough target now," Nitin groaned.

"No no… it's too early to pass such comments, let's watch," I said quickly.

"Let's bet on it," Nitin exhorted and patted the centre table.

I thought for a second and said, "Okay, if India wins, I want to attend your engagement party before I leave."

"Oh god! You have been after our lives... could you keep your nose out of this, can't you! For some time at least, please!" Nitin grumbled. I hung my head glumly. But he melted seeing my puppy face, "Okay, I will," he said. His announcement made everyone look at him surprised.

"And if I win the bet, you have to promise you will settle down in India soon," he smartly put the clause. That was less the clause, but more a wish which everyone had in their heart; me too.

Whatever the bet was, the two girls were very happy; it was in their favour.

The match became interesting gradually. India got a stable partnership. It was 140 runs in 25 overs after one wicket down. Virender had scored 88 runs. Would he score a century was the excitement. In the 27th over, the Sri Lankan bowler Murali Dharan took the field. Suddenly, Nitin screamed in excitement, "If he makes his century, I will talk to my parents today only, about us, I bet!" On the 5th ball of the over, Virender hit for a boundary and completed his century. Neha ran to Nitin and gave him a kiss; that match had made her day after all. India won by four wickets in hand, and with that, I also won my bet. Now Nitin was bound to the promise he had made, that he would be engaged to Neha before I leave India.

On 17 March 2009, Richa and I got married, and on 22 March, Nitin and Neha exchanged rings.

With so many sweet memories, I left India with Richa. In July, Nitin and Neha also got married.

PART II

We never imagined that whatever we had started just for our joy would lead to a tough time for all of us. Betting, which had brought happiness to Neha and Nitin's life, would also take away our happiness one day.

"We'll land in New Delhi in a few minutes… passengers are requested to fasten their seat belts…" The air hostess's voice brought me back to the present. Richa was sleeping, her head on my shoulder. I woke her up.

"Oh… have we reached?" she asked, rubbing her eyes, and put the seat belt on.

The rear wheels touched the runway. The jolt inside the aircraft made me felt associated to my land, where my soul was.

My family had come to pick us up at the airport. I asked about Gourav's health. He was still critical, they said. I requested them to drop me at the hospital. But, it was already dark outside. Mom wanted me to come home first, but my patience was wearing thin; I wanted to see Gourav eagerly. Ultimately, they had to drop me at the hospital.

Inside the hospital, I saw Shalini sitting with her mother-in-law in front of the ICU. They looked pale and tired. Gourav's mother was sitting in a wheel chair, looking thinner than when I last saw her. His father was talking to the doctor; I went over to listen to what the doctor was saying.

"The surgeons are trying their best, but bleeding is uncontrollable now, we need more blood immediately," the doctor said and went inside the ICU.

Seeing me beside him, Gourav's father asked, "Amit! When did you come to India?"

"Today, uncle."

Uncle held my shoulder and narrated the entire incident to me, the same thing that Nitin had told me before. He said that Nitin had gone to the blood bank to get some more bottles of blood. Gourav's blood group was AB^+ and it was not available at the hospital at that time.

Aunty sniffed and looked woebegone; Shailni was squeezing her hand gently. I was watching them helplessly. I pacified them for a while and stood beside them.

Meanwhile, Nitin came and handed the bottles to the doctor. I went to him, we hugged tightly, and our eyes became wet. Nitin had been in the hospital for the last two days; he found solace in having me around.

"How was your journey? Are you coming directly from the airport?" he asked.

"Yeah, could not wait till tomorrow," I said.

After a pause, I asked, "How did all this happen? And who were the people who stabbed him?"

"Police is investigating. He has made lots of enemies in the past few months."

"What do you mean by 'he made enemies'?" I asked confused.

"The police suspect that the mafia or some gangsters could be behind this. The way he came forward to help the police in the match-fixing scandals, many people had him on their radar. You might not be aware about what is going on in this country, but all the match-fixing scandals are coming in light. Police and ACSU are hot on their trail. Some players and big names from the business world have been found culpable. Involvement of underworld and mafia has already been proved. The police has raided many illegal bookmaking centres and arrested a number of bookies. Many of them have the protection of the underworld and are hiding in other countries," Nitin said.

We talked for some more time. Nitin kept telling me about the past few months. I looked at my watch; it was 10 p.m.

Nitin insisted I leave. Rajeev was also reaching the next morning.

But I wanted to see Gourav once before leaving. On my request, the doctor allowed me into the ICU. Surrounded with several machines and tubes, I saw Gourav enveloped in white gauze and bandage all over his body. The beeps coming from the ECG was the only noise disturbing the tranquillity of the forlorn room. He was still, no sign of movement. The oxygen mask had left his face partially visible from a distance. I stared at him for a while, praying to see him smile at me soon.

Gambling: An addiction

There has always been a thin line between habit and addiction, and if crossed, a habit can easily turn into an addiction. A fun filled harmless want creeps up slowly into a compulsive craving, unknowingly sticking its neck out.

Rajeev, Gourav and Nitin used to meet when a cricket match was afoot and always bet to add more euphoria to the experience. Gradually, betting became second nature to them and was not limited to the three friends only. Steadily, it was spreading out. Nitin used to bet with his colleagues on matches during his office hours.

And then, the Cricket World Cup began. Nitin's enthusiasm was at its peak. He had also asked Rajeev and Gourav to participate in betting over the phone during office hours. This new trend fanned their hobby in the direction where they might sail close to the wind.

Gradually, Nitin became the nucleus. He was accepting the bets of others and paying out money. Initially, it could not get through his head that he has turned into a bookie. Majority of people were sticking together in the betting game. Sometimes he would find himself unable to handle the situation; and asked Rajeev and Gourav to help him out in handling wagers.

Systematically, they divided the workload with everyone's consent. Rajeev was monitoring the flow of money, Nitin was taking care of the persons involved in betting and their bets, and Gourav was keeping track of the game and related betting results.

This had become their part-time job and was obtaining professionalism day by day. Soon they set their bookmaking office in Gourav's flat, he was living alone. After office hours, they used to meet at Gourav's place and together they sorted out the transactions.

One evening, Mr Ramakant Kesari called up Gourav. Mr Kesari was the marketing manager at the pharmaceuticals company where Gourav worked. Not untouched of the betting fever, he was a punter and had been in contact with Gourav and his group over the last few days. He had put his bet on cricket through them twice, and had won.

He had called to put a bet on the match happening the next day. The betting amount was Rs 3 lakhs; it was the first time that they were dealing with such a large amount. But against expectations, the match proved an awful shock to Mr Kesari; he lost the bet. Losing huge money was a bitter pill to swallow. That burst his bubble, and he became furious. Ultimately, Gourav fall prey of his manifest disappointment and frustration.

Gourav's performance in office was not up to the mark from last three to four months. He was not focused on his work. Mr Kesari noticed that. He asked Gourav's immediate boss, the Group Product Manager, to check out Gourav's performance. Gourav was working under him as a Product Manager, and already had got warnings from him several times. This time, the management declared him a futile resource and asked him to leave the company. Gourav resigned and left the job.

"Gourav, what's next?" Rajeev asked Gourav when they met in the evening. "I fetched some of my contacts; you can get good recommendation in Sanofi India or Glenmark."

Gourav was sitting on his bed, his back against the wall. He drew heavily on his cigarette and puffed out a cloud of smoke, then said coldly, "I have also sorted some companies where I can try, but you know what? I am losing interest in doing a job; the same boring grunt work every day. Want to flee from this dull drudgery."

Nitin sprang up from the couch and grumbled, "It's all because of Mr Kesari. Damn, what does he think of himself? It's all luck. Sometimes you win, and sometimes you don't… it's all luck man. The time when he was winning, he didn't have any grievances with Gourav, but as soon he turned into red, suddenly Gourav became the worst performer in his team. The swine…!"

Rajeev sat in front of Gourav and patted him consolingly and said, "Neglect it like a nightmare, it happens in corporate life. Don't let yourself down because of this trivial episode. Just step forward and get back to the drawing board."

"No, no, you guys misconstrued. I really don't have any hard feelings for Mr Kesari or… anyone else. The thing is, now-a-days I do not like to work under someone's authority. All this makes me dull and pissed off… I don't find any ball of fire in me. I want to work for myself, which could keep me motivated and elated," Gourav said and smashed the cigarette butt in the ash-tray calmly.

For a while, the room was totally quiet. Nitin and Rajeev were looking at Gourav unexpectedly. Gourav looked at them, the curious two pairs of eyes staring at him had questions, and among those one had even done his homework and brought recommendations for his new job. He has to be clear and specific to them and speak his mind.

"I wish to establish my own business. Where only I would be all-in-all, and not anyone else would be my boss. My uphill battle would be for myself and not for some third person. I already have completed my Diploma in Pharmacy." Cutting to the chase, Gourav came to his main point, "I want to set up a chemist shop."

Both of them were listening to him patiently. "Not a bad idea! It's good, really good! In fact, your degree and your experience will be used here," Rajeev encouraged him.

"Buddy! If you have made up your mind and have confidence, then nothing is better than owning your own business! Whatever help you want from us, just tell us, we are always with you," Nitin said.

A smile appeared on Gourav's face. "Thank for your support and encouragement. But, something is bothering me too. I'm not sure if I'm taking the right decision. What happens if I don't have success in business or if it gets ruined after some years? There is so much risk involved, you know," his face turned tensed with this.

Rajeev looked concerned, and said, "Your worry is obvious, Gourav. It happens before taking an important decision. There is some calculated risk involved, but you will have to go through this risk; only then you can get the fruit. What will happen or what will not, leave it to time and have faith in yourself. You just work hard. Your goal is in front of you and it will shape up according to your will only."

After Rajeev's enlightened speech, Nitin also felt that he should say something impressive. "Rajeev is right, Gourav. You should at least give it a try and put your best foot forward. Always remember, every dark cloud has a silver lining."

Rajeev and Gourav laughed. "Thank you so much for encouraging me. Your views and advice mean a lot to me," Gourav said and hugged them both. "I need funds to establish my shop at first and support of you guys as well."

"Aah! We have genie! No problem. All we need is to brush the magical lamp intelligently. This bookmaking is bestowing us a good return. Let's invest a handsome sum of money, and then we could look for a good location to start the business. What say?" Nitin asked.

A new start

Gourav short-listed some places. After discussion, they finalised the shop location in Vasant Kunj near Fortis hospital. For this, they needed two crore rupees. Apart from this, supplies of drugs, renovation, lighting, furniture and fixtures would cost another handsome sum of money.

Now Gourav had a clear aim of setting up his business and betting was the channel to reach his aim.

However, Gourav's parents were very upset about his decision. His father wanted him to continue with his job rather than to start a new business. He tried to convince him many times, that the path he had chosen to reach his goal wouldn't help him by any means, and circumstances would make him a mere spiv. But every time, Gourav tried his utmost to convey the importance of bookmaking in making money to his parent.

With Rajeev's help, Gourav got a loan for his shop from his bank.

Next step was to get a licence for his shop. He went to the drug controller office with Nitin to fill the forms. Nitin found it to be a tedious work, as there were a number of documents that had to be attached along with the application form. Gourav saw Nitin yawning while going through the checklist. He asked Nitin to come outside and have some tea or coffee. "It's not possible to deposit this form today." Nitin said.

"Don't worry, I have some contacts, I'll get it done soon," said Gourav. "What would you like to have?"

"Cold coffee I think," Nitin said and sank into a sofa.

Gourav came back with two cold coffees.

"What do you say? How much time will it take?"

"A few weeks. After that, the drug inspector will inspect the premises of the shop, and at the time of inspection, the store must be ready with furniture and fixtures. If he is satisfied, our licence will be issued," Gourav said and took a sip of the coffee.

"Do you think the process is easy?"

"Not really, but as I told you, I have contacts. My ex-colleague Raman knows some touts in the drug controller's office. Through him, I could get all my paper-work done. Generally, these touts are always in contact with drug inspectors, so all the work will be done on time. And most of the time, money wins the show," Gourav said and readjusted himself on the sofa.

"Bribe… don't know when our country will be better," Nitin said satirically and put his empty glass on the table.

"Let's go, we have lots of work to do. Mamaji has given contact numbers of some carpenters. I have to meet them today itself and finalise," Gourav said and tried to spring up from the sofa.

Gourav had been working his finger to the bone to set up his business. With the help of touts he completed his paper-work and deposited it at the office. Renovation work had started, and not a single corner was untouched of Gourav's skilful interior advice. Finally the day came when the drug inspector of that area happened to visit the proposed premises of the shop. Gourav was well prepared; he checked several times that everything was in its place. The drug inspector made a note of everything and looked quite convinced. After inspecting every aspect, he left, satisfied. And a few days later, Gourav got the licence for his shop.

His next step was to get suppliers. And soon he found some decent suppliers in Ghaziabad. Gourav was taking advantage of his previous job, and was able to fetch good discounts on medicines.

Raman, his colleague; had told him to meet one Diwakar Aggarwal, who had been running a pharmacy for a long time and could give Gourav some tips. So Gourav and Rajeev went to meet Mr Diwakar at his residence in the afternoon.

A tall middle-aged man opened the door, wearing white kurta-pyjama and spectacles.

"Yes….?" he asked, adjusting his specs.

"Mr Diwakar?" Gourav asked.

"Yes, it's me."

"I am Gourav, Raman might have told you about me."

"Oh, yes, yes. You were working with him in his company, right? Come in, come, come," and he let them in.

"Please sit," he indicated to the sofa.

"Raman had told me that you are opening your own medical shop," Mr Diwakar said.

"Yes, it will open soon; it's in Vasant Kunj near Fortis hospital."

Meanwhile, a teen-aged boy came and served cold water. Both picked up their glasses.

"Raman told me that you have been in this business for quite a long time. And I am the new kid on the block. If you could share your experiences and advice, I will be grateful to you. I need your tips and guidance," Gourav said humbly.

Mr Diwakar felt glad to hear that someone wanted his advice and guidance. He nodded and asked, "Okay, tell me what you want to know." And simultaneously he asked the boy to bring some snacks and cold drinks for them.

"A general assumption is that the profit margin in this business is not very high. So, how do I deal with this factor?" Gourav asked.

"Hmm, see, the margin depends upon the type of sales you are doing. Type 1 is sale of prescription drugs. Here, the margin stands at about 20%. Some shopkeepers increase their margins by replacing the branded drugs with generic drugs on which the margin is very high. But remember that this is unethical practice and will harm you in the long run. Type 2 is direct sales. In this, a person comes to you and asks for medicines for certain general disorders, like cough, cold, fever, etc. The chemist almost dispenses generic medicines to such patients. A bottle of cough syrup should not cost you more than Rs 5-7 and it will fetch you about Rs 60. Ten bottles a day and you are set. Surgical items have a margin beyond imagination. A product with an MRP of Rs. 100 might cost you just Rs.10. MRP on surgical items is always quoted a lot more than it costs a chemist, so even if you provide a discount of 30-35%, it's not going to affect you. You won't believe that a crepe bandage priced at 150 could be bought for Rs 25 from the wholesale market." Mr Diwakar said.

Rajeev's throat choked on his drink when he heard the margin of price in wholesale market and retail market. He put his glass on the table and coughed to clear his throat. "Excuse me, but is it true?" he asked.

Mr Diwakar smiled. "A generic injection of Amikacin costs Rs 7-9 and a branded one costs Rs 54. Well, both are equally effective. Now fix your margin and sell it at Rs 25-30. The customer will get it at a much lower price and you will get a high margin. If you can make people understand that both are equally effective, you will make your day. Giving good discounts is the key to attract attention initially. It acts as viral marketing and people flock in, and turnover becomes the game player here. Free home delivery for monthly medical calls, order on phone for regular clients, client membership card discounts, etc., are also some hot methods. Rapport with hospitals, clinics, etc., gives additional benefits. You might have to sell things at cost or even at loss to them, but bulk orders give you a big benefit in getting better discounts from suppliers. Remember, turnover is a game changer.

"Charge the supplier for display space and for promotional activities. Keep lots of change; it always helps in retaining customers. Collect various medical guides available from suppliers, like diabetes monthly chart or pregnancy charts, etc. Give these away for free. This is generally dumped in the distributor's stock room. Giving these as gifts to clients makes them happy, as it's unexpected."

That was a lot of information, and I was lost in thoughts. "Please have some pakode with this green chutney. It's delicious,

I tell you," Mr Diwakar said, then continued his advices and ideas.

They stayed for an hour, then thanked him for sharing his valuable advice and experience, and took his leave. Mr Diwakar came to the gate to see them off and asked them to visit again.

"Wasn't it worth coming here?" Rajeev said, starting his bike.

"Doubtlessly, it was. I'm more confident now after meeting Mr Diwakar. Let's meet suppliers now," Gourav said.

And Rajeev rode the bike in the direction to meet the suppliers next.

They got a mentor

Triangular series was around the corner. The participants were India, Pakistan and South Africa; the matches were to be hosted by India and Pakistan. The three friends were all set to conduct the betting game. This time, they raised the stakes. Every punter would have to put up Rs 45,000. Their bets would be recorded for proof, and punters could stake a claim only after the end of the series.

One day, Nitin's colleague introduced him to a punter named Mohamad Ajeez. Ajeez was a well-established businessman in Pakistan. He was in India for business. He wanted to bet a good amount on the tournament.

After some time, Nitin came to know that he was also connected with some Pakistani bookies; through them, he was placing bets in Pakistan. Nitin discussed that with his friends. And lastly they concluded that they had nothing to do with that as it was Ajeez's personal interest. Anyway, it wouldn't affect their business at all.

In that tournament, Ajeez won Rs 3.5 lakhs from them. He called them to his hotel for coffee. Rajeev, Nitin and Gourav went to the hotel with the money. Ajeez had instructed the receptionist to send the boys to the coffee corner.

Ajeez was waiting for them, clad in a white kurta-pyjama. He had a French beard and spectacles, and was reading a newspaper.

"Hello sir!" they greeted him.

"Oh! Come, come, I was waiting for you guys," Ajeez signalled them to sit.

Nitin handed over the winning amount to him. "Congratulations, sir, it's all yours," he said.

Ajeez grinned, took the packet. "It's all luck," he said, and ordered four cups of coffee.

"So for how many days are you here, sir?" Nitin asked.

"Just for one more week, then I will leave for Bangladesh. I am in the business of gems and diamonds and often travel across the neighbouring countries. I like to meet new people and make new friends. My family is in Pakistan."

The three of them smiled and nodded. "Now you tell me what you all do apart from bookmaking," Ajeez asked.

"Rajeev and I both work in a bank and Gourav has recently quit his job and will start his own business very soon," Nitin said.

"It is good. How did you boys get into bookmaking?" Ajeez asked.

Meanwhile, a waiter came with four mugs of piping hot coffee and carefully placed them on the table.

"We gradually got involved. At first, we were doing it for fun and eventually it became our passion," Nitin said.

'And now it has become a necessity,' Gourav thought to himself and picked up the coffee mug.

"Around ten-twelve years ago, I was also like you. I was passionate about bookmaking; it was like an addiction for me. But later, I decided to get away from it and I left," Ajeez said nostalgically.

"Why did you leave?" Rajeev asked, putting the coffee mug back on the table.

"I had the liability of my family. My father died in an accident. I had two young sisters and my mother. I took over the business; Ammi assisted me in that. Ammi had to do most of the work as I used to spend most of the time in bookmaking. Ammi's health was deteriorating gradually. Suddenly, in the year 2000, the match-fixing scandal came into the limelight. The Hansie Cronje tapes were released by Delhi Police, the police was alert and raids were taking place, so many illegal bookies were arrested. The ICC (International Cricket Council) suspended several players. The whole world knows who they were. These things shook me. I destroyed every bit of evidence of my bookmaking business. I was scared what would happen if the police caught me. My family name would be spoiled forever. After me, who would take care of my family? Ammi was already feeble. I decided that I should take the whole responsibility of the business, and she should take rest. After that, I left bookmaking and focused on my family business." He had a look of nostalgia in his eyes, his face was set hard.

"But betting is my hobby. I do it for myself. I can't tear myself away from cricket. So I still bet my money on this silly game." Ajeez grinned and took some sips of his coffee.

"Do you ever regret losing a huge amount?" asked Rajeev.

"Dear, this is a gamble. Sometimes you win and sometimes you lose. It's all luck. When luck gives, then it has all the right to take back from you. Yes, I have lost, so many times. Whatever I earned from you guys, it's possible you could get it all the next time from me." Ajeez was laughing.

"You guys are young and new to this. I would like to share my experience with you boys. I have seen this world up close. It is based on trust. If the customer doesn't trust you or you don't trust them, then there is no business. Bookmaking is illegal here, but trustworthiness is its core value. A general assumption is that it's shadowy. But it is the fairest business, I think. It's quite clear until someone tampers; he might be a bookie, or punter or anyone else. They manipulate things in their favour, which is wrong. Match fixing and spot fixing has tattered the bookmaking business.

"What I will suggest is, be fair in your business and play safe, be alert every time. Cheating, bad contacts, involvement in scandals can raise troubles for you, and then things can get worse and dangerous, my dear," Ajeez said.

For a few seconds, a deep silence prevailed. Rajeev broke it when he said, "Sir, your views and advice are precious to us. We are really grateful that you shared it with us."

As they finished their coffee, Gourav invited Mr Ajeez to the opening of his chemist shop.

"I'll come, dear. My blessings are with you. I am happy that you are starting your own business. It's very important, not to let bookmaking be your career. Let it be just another source of earning, but not the main source. And limit it to just a hobby and not your passion. Always remember these things," said Ajeez.

The chemist shop, which was the big motive behind this illegal business, was finally all set to be inaugurated. 'Nirmal Medicals' was the name of the shop. Close friends and relatives came to give their blessings to Gourav on his new start. Gourav smashed a coconut in front of his shop and called his mother forward to cut the ribbon.

Cricketer cum brother

Vivek Mishra, a right-handed batsman, was a rising star in the Indian cricket team. In Ranji, he drew the attention of the selectors by hitting 4 half centuries and 3 centuries. After that, he played for the ICC Under-19 cricket world cup. He proved his potential through his strike rate of 68 and was selected to play international cricket.

Vivek and Gourav were cousins. Their fathers were partners in a cane furniture business in Bareilly, a city in Uttar Pradesh. Their childhood was spent in Bareilly. They used to go to school together and after school, they used to play cricket in the playground located between their house and school.

After a few years, their parents decided to expand their business, so Vivek's father moved to Chandigarh along with his family. In Chandigarh, Vivek got involved in cricket, and played several matches at the school level. Seeing his interest in cricket, his father allowed him to join a cricket academy. There, he got a good opportunity to polish his batting skills. Very soon, at thirteen, he played for his state. His practice, dedication and passion put him on the path to success, and now he was playing for his country.

It was like a dream come true for his parents. I remember how happy Gourav was when Vivek played his first international against West Indies; he had spent a large portion of his pocket money on giving a treat to his friends. It was the first time I had tasted beer. I felt that it was bitter, but celebration was in the air and I enjoyed drinking. Gourav had always been in touch with him, and because of that, Rajeev and Nitin also got the opportunity to meet him.

When Gourav involved himself in bookmaking, he started taking advantage of his relationship with Vivek off and on, by making him give information about the condition of the pitch, who would play and who would not, whether anyone was unfit or injured. This information provided him vital clues, which aided him in the game of betting.

Problems do not knock

Gourav now had his own shop and he got engrossed in that. He had hired three sales persons for assistance, so that if he was busy in bookmaking, they could handle the shop. But it seemed his luck was also playing hide-and-seek with him. His mother had not been well for a few weeks and her medical report revealed she had cervical cancer. His parents came to Delhi for further check-ups. He took his mother to Rajeev Gandhi Cancer Institute and Research Centre. The doctors declared that the cancer had reached the second stage. Gourav decided that all further treatments would be done in the same hospital, and that they would stay with him in his flat.

Rajeev and Nitin shifted their bookmaking centre from Gourav's house to a rented accommodation, their new so-called office. Now the main work load was on Rajeev and Nitin as Gourav's first priority was his mother's treatment. He had also left his shop to his salesmen. He would go to the shop only once in two to three days.

The doctors had said that the size of tumour was about four cm. it was recommended to give her brachytherapy and external radiation therapy.

The treatment was pretty expensive, and the treatment had shaken the family's financial stability.

His father's cane furniture business was sinking in his absence. Somehow Gourav's mamaji was taking care of the business in both Bareilly and Chandigarh. For Gourav's father, it was not possible to leave his wife in that condition and go back to business again. So he decided to close the shop and split from the partnership.

'*10 people died and 9 are critical in the city after taking spurious medicines. In the last three days, the number of patients in hospitals has increased, and according to the doctors, they have had severe reactions on taking some fake medicines. Police has woken up after two days and is now investigating the whole issue.*' The news was continuously flashing across all channels.

The victims, in their statements to the police, had named several chemist shops, including Nirmal Medicals. The Police raided the shop, and Gourav was caught unawares. Police confiscated the stock which was suspected to be poisonous and sealed the shop. The next day, the report came from the lab and the drugs were proven poisonous. Gourav was arrested for further interrogation.

Gourav was unaware of the facts. In fact, he had delegated the task of dealing with distributors and monitoring the stock to one of his sales people. He denied all the allegations. He named the suppliers from whom he bought the drugs. The police raided the supplier, and very soon, the entire chain of drugs mafia was in the police's hand.

Gourav was charged with selling poisonous drugs to the public, but without knowing so. He was found innocent in this case and only charged a penalty.

But the entire episode had affected his reputation in the market. One day, Mr Diwakar Agarwal called up Gourav. "I heard your shop was raided for fake and poisonous drugs. Is it true?"

"How did you know that?" Gourav asked, surprised.

"Bad news travels fast," Mr Diwakar said.

"It's all the result of negligence, I could say. My mother is hospitalised and I couldn't give sufficient time to my pharmacy. For the last three months, my sales boys have been taking care of the entire business. Some distributors took advantage of that situation and supplied those fake drugs to my shop. I came to know only when the police raided my shop. That is all," Gourav moaned.

"Oh! By the way, it is very difficult to differentiate between genuine medicines and fake ones. And an untrained person could never find out. From where do you get your supplies?" Mr Diwakar asked.

"I have some suppliers from Ghaziabad and also some authorised distributors who used to visit time to time."

"I should have told you before that Ghaziabad and Agra are notorious for fake medicines. I would advise you to go to Bhagirath Palace, which is a hub of drugs wholesalers. Some of them know me very well; you can give them my references also. Be careful the next time, bad publicity in our business is not good. It could ruin our reputation in the market."

Mr Diwakar was right. Bad publicity could never help in this business. Nirmal Medicals had become an untrustworthy name among the customers. The number of clients fell day by day; per day sales became very low. Gourav had already taken orders on credit from the distributors, and now it seemed difficult to pay their bills also. Gourav was in debt. He was now finding it difficult to meet the expenses of his mother's treatment, the bank loan, and bills of suppliers. In this situation, bookmaking was the only ray of hope, but it was also not capable of meeting all the requirements, because among the three partners, no one was devoting quality time to it. Rajeev and Nitin were running busy in their office and could spare only a little time for bookmaking. Gourav had also been shuttling between bookmaking, his pharmacy and the hospital. His mama used to visit from time to time and stealthily give some money to his brother-in-law for his sister's treatment.

Gourav had not paid the EMI against his loan to the bank since the last five months. The bank kept sending him notifications from time to time. Gourav informed the bank about his financial hardship, and begged for some more time to make payments of the entire outstanding amount.

Gourav's mother was lying on the bed when his father came in with some medicines and a glass of water. Gourav came in with her meal and kept the plate on the side table. "How are you feeling now, Maa?" he asked while going towards the windows to close them and adjust the curtain.

"Having some mild pain, but that's bearable. You tell me, how was your day?" Gourav gave her a fake smile. "You are looking very weak, are you eating properly? I doubt it. Come sit beside me for some time," she moaned.

"I wish Maa, but I am getting late. I have to reach office. Rajeev and Nitin will be there. Will talk to you later," Gourav gave her a light hug and left.

"I am worried about him. He is looking very tense these days," she said. "Has he told you anything? How is his business going? Any improvement in customers?" she asked, looking at her husband. When she didn't get any response from him, she lamented, "No one says anything to me." Her eyes got moist.

Seeing her anxiety, he came to her and said desperately, "What can I say? Business is risky; it is not easy for everyone. I spent working really hard in my business; you know that there are ups and downs. That's why I always wished that my son would get a good education and employment in a reputed company, which could secure his future. I told him not to leave his job; not to leave the service sector, it will be a bad decision… but no, he didn't listen to me. Established his own business and… and how? By taking a huge loan from the bank. Now he suffers with that."

"He is our child, we can't leave him on his own at this bad time. Can't you see he doesn't speak much at home. I am worried about him. It's a time when we should be with him, to hold his hand and tell him he is not alone. If a child makes a mistake, the parent's duty is to show him the right path, rather than to curse. And it is not fair to blame him; my illness is also responsible for the crisis. It has financially drained both of you. Otherwise, everything was in place." She groaned, "You should talk to Gourav and pacify him."

"All right... all right, I will talk to him, but first, you have your food. You have to take more medication after this." He brought the plate in front of her.

That night, Gourav came late. After dinner, he went to his room. Sitting on his bed, he was looking at the starry sky when his father came inside.

"You haven't slept yet?" his father asked.

"No papa, just not sleepy." Gourav turned towards him.

"You seem very low. All these incidents have made you restless, haven't they? You have lost your peace, my son. Something is bothering you, isn't it? Please tell me." He came near him and sat on the bed.

Gourav hung his head and lamented, "I am finding it difficult to run the shop now, and customers have lost their trust. My business is in huge loss. I am thinking of shutting down this business now."

His father yelled out in shock. "What? Are you nuts? This shop was your dream! Don't do this, my dear. How could just one failure make you so fragile?"

Gourav lamented, "Business can't be run in loss, papa."

"If you remember, I told you in the beginning that risk is always involved in business. But you were firm on your decision, because you had faith in yourself. In the past, whatever allegations you faced were just because you were not alert. Always remember, an alert mind averts the danger, even in adverse situations. Now, take it as a lesson and be strong, bring some positivity in yourself. Ups and downs are the nature of business, what you have to do is try your best to take your business up. Put your best foot forward. Did you think of recovering the trust of customers, of building a good image in the market?" his father asked.

Gourav shook his head. "What should I do now?"

"Change the name of your shop, because the controversy is related to the name. And bring some changes in the shop's look, if possible. Bring positivity in your attitude; be more convincing to your customers. And don't worry about your mother. I will take care of her, as she is quite stable now. You concentrate upon your business; it needs your quality time. Trust is the backbone of your business; never let it go. I have faith in god; you will get back all that you have lost." His father egged him on.

"Thanks, papa," Gourav held his father's hand in his hands. "Your encouragement and belief mean a lot to me, papa."

His father smiled, ruffled his hair, and said, "We also have our ancestral land. I have thought that in the worst case, I will sell it off. Now try to sleep, it's late."

Gourav did as his father told him. The new name he kept for his shop was 'Prayag Medicals', and he tried to give it a new look. Gradually, people came to like his polite and helping behaviour.

But the main problem was to pay the bank loan. One month had passed and not enough funds were collected yet. The bank took legal action against Gourav. Debt Recovery Tribunal sent a notice to him. In the hearing, Gourav informed the bank about all the problems and asked for some more time and pledged to pay all his dues. Considering his reasons and looking at the past track record of his EMI repayment, the bank finally offered him a leeway, and gave him sixty more days.

Though selling his ancestral land would fetch a handsome amount, it was his last hope, but he didn't want to sell it off. He just couldn't, because there were so many emotions of his parents attached to that land. He had to do something else… but what?

A daring decision

The 'Titan cup' one-day international cricket series was going to be held in a few days.

The three friends were sitting together watching the news on television at Nitin's house.

"We have an opportunity to make some money in this series," Gourav said.

Rajeev changed the news channel and switched to MTV. "That's true Gourav, but it's dicey. We can, if luck will be with us, but who knows about luck?"

"But betting is the only way, it seems, to make money. I have a wicked plan to put the ball in our court. Hey Rajeev, please mute the TV," Nitin asked Rajeev.

"Oh-o, I like the lyrics of the song. Can't you wait till it finishes?" Rajeev said, ignoring his request. Nitin looked at him, infuriated. "Okay, okay, I could lower the volume. Now reveal your black-hearted plan, what is it?" Rajeev asked.

"Vivek… he can help us in winning bets," Nitin said and looked at their faces.

"You want to manipulate the game?" Rajeev asked, surprised.

"I am only talking about Vivek's performance in the coming series. We can talk to him. I know he will understand our problem," Nitin clarified.

"I don't agree with you. Till now, we have played fair in this business. What you are talking about is deceiving our customers," Rajeev argued. "Gourav, what do you say, don't you think it's wrong?" Rajeev asked.

Gourav thought for a while, evaluating all the 'ifs and buts' in his mind, and then said, "Rajeev, I need money. The bank has given me sixty days; already seven days have passed. Now I have only fifty-three days in hand. I have to arrange twelve lakh rupees for the bank, else it will seize my shop. Also, I am in the thick of debt and have to arrange for mom's treatment expenses. What Nitin is saying is wrong, I know, but this is the only way left for us."

"You guys have gone crazy. You might get into trouble. If your father has told you he will sell off his land, then why are you so panicked?" Rajeev raised his point.

"That is our ancestral land, Rajeev, where my forefathers used to farm. I have spent my childhood in those fields. I know it won't be easy for papa to sell it off. And it is the only property we have. How could I let it go so easily for paying my debts? I must try something else. I hope you understand," Gourav said, looking into Rajeev's eyes.

Nitin said, "We should take a chance for the sake of friendship. Don't you remember the slogan we learnt in school 'a friend in need is a friend indeed'...*haann?*"

That was enough to drive Rajeev to the edge. Rajeev gave Nitin a knuckle sandwich on his belly.

"Aaaaooo!" Nitin screamed. "Take it easy, man. I was just trying to convince you that we should do something for him, the poor boy," he told Rajeev.

"You both have made up your mind. Now whatever I'll say will go in vain. And how come all the corrupt and evil thoughts come to your brain only?" Rajeev glared at Nitin. "You were the one who started all this betting syndicate, and now are ready to take a leap into match fixing. Hmm, I doubt you sometimes," Rajeev groaned.

"Match-fixing…Ooo," Nitin put his fingers to his mouth. "What are you talking about, Rajeev? Match-fixing is a very big thing. I am just talking about Vivek, he is like our brother. If he is ready to help Gourav, what is wrong? And let's assume it is wrong. So what? It is just a game, an entertainment factor. People like to bet their surplus money, which doesn't affect their living. And remember, we are doing it for a genuine cause," Nitin said nobly.

Rajeev wanted to punch him hard this time, but before he did, Gourav announced, "I've decided. I'll take this chance. I will talk to Vivek. Let's see how he takes our proposal."

Gourav called Vivek and asked him to meet up at a mall.

Next day, Vivek and Gourav met at a coffee shop.

"Is everything all right? How is *bua* now?" Vivek asked.

Gourav told him about his mother's health and also let him know about all the ups and downs he had faced in the last few months. "Vivek, I have told you everything. You can understand that I am in crisis. I need your help. I hope you won't say no," Gourav said.

"Tell me, how can I help you?" Vivek said.

Then Gourav told him about his plan of spot fixing. And for that, he would pay him around 40% of the earnings. At first, Vivek hesitated, but at last Gourav convinced Vivek to play for him in the coming series. So Gourav gave him a mobile on which they could talk during the series. Also, they fixed some code words so that they could talk without arousing suspicion.

Rajeev didn't think it was ethical. He tried to convince Gourav and Nitin against it, but all in vain. He was stuck between the devil and the deep sea; on one side, his close friends and on the other side, his moral principles. The way that his partners had chosen did not seem convincing to him. At last he heard his inner voice and decided to part ways from the partnership.

The first match was between South Africa and England. Gourav and Nitin were seated in their so-called office with their equipment. Gourav was keeping track of the odds whereas Nitin was recording bets of the customers. It went without saying that they missed Rajeev's company. But they also knew that once the series ended and all the problems were sorted out, they would get Rajeev back.

The next match was between England and India. The day before the match, Gourav called up Vivek on the mobile which he had given to him.

"Tomorrow, the car won't go beyond twenty km," Gourav said.

"Only twenty?" Vivek asked.

"Petrol price is rising high, my brother," Gourav said.

"Okay," Vivek said.

Here, Gourav had told Vivek in code words that he should not score more than twenty runs. Punters were betting high on him.

Next day, when the match started, India won the toss and opted for batting. The first wicket fell in the 6th over on 32 runs. Then Vivek came to the crease for batting. He made eighteen runs in twenty-two balls and on his twenty-third ball, he recklessly got run out. The audience was shocked; he was playing well, then why did he try to take an unnecessarily risky run? The commentator criticised his deplorable play.

Gourav won a good amount in betting and made his punters feel low. Both Nitin and Gourav celebrated that night. Their plan had worked.

In the rest of the series also, Vivek played as Gourav asked him to play. And thus, when the series ended, Gourav had won a big amount.

At the end of the series, Gourav and Nitin earned Rs 8.40 lakhs, out of which he had to pay Rs 3.36 lakhs to Vivek.

"I'll ask Vivek to lend his share to us for some time and we will pay him later in instalments. I know he will understand my condition," Gourav told Nitin.

"Don't do that; give him his money. See, by taking his money, our problem won't get solved. We still need four lakhs more. Vivek is our trump card; he shouldn't feel that he is doing some kind of charity work for us. Every player loves money; the money will encourage him to play further for us. Got it?" Nitin expounded his idea.

"I agree with you. But in that case, money is still an issue," Gourav calculated.

"Not exactly. If you remember, next month, the Asia cup is going to be held in Sri Lanka. We still have some chance, my dear," Nitin said in excitement.

Gourav understood Nitin's indication and decided to talk to Vivek further.

Together we can make more money

Gourav was standing in the front of Vivek's house, with a white packet in hand. He paused for a minute before pressing the door bell and looked at the packet again. Was he really going to ask him for further help? But who would risk his career in the name of 'help' again and again. Nitin was right; he should talk professionally to Vivek, and make him agree to the deal. With a fresh resolve, he rang the door bell. Vivek's mother opened the door.

Vivek greeted her and asked, "Where is Vivek?"

"He is taking a shower. Entered home just ten minutes back," his Mamiji said, and asked about his mother's health.

"She is stable for the time being, treatment is in continuation. Next week she has radiation therapy again," Gourav said.

"Aaah… she is a kind woman, such a nice and gentle soul. Why has god written such kind of suffering for her," she lamented.

By that time, Vivek's father had come into the living room too, and changed the TV channel from Star Plus to Star Sports. The highlights of Titan Cup cricket match series, India vs England were playing. And Vivek was batting.

The channel showed Vivek's run out on the score of eighteen, also replayed thrice to have a better analysis. It showed so clearly how recklessly he had lost his wicket. Mamaji seemed upset. "See, how he is playing international cricket. Taking such irresponsible calls. Was there a need of that risk? He would have scored seventy plus, or perhaps even a century if he had not played so childishly. Sometimes nobody can understand what he does."

"Ohho, let it be. Why are you getting upset? It happens sometime. You enjoy *dahi-vade*," and Mamiji passed another bowl to Mamaji.

Mamaji didn't stop, "Why shouldn't I? The apple of your eye has reached that far because I have put my hard savings on his trainings. He can't play blindly," he said and dug into the first bite.

"How do you know the pressure he handles in the ground. It is easy to comment sitting on the sofa and slurping dahi-vade," Mamiji came forward to defend her boy.

Gourav was listening to them, and froze. His hands were stuck with the spoon in mid-air, between his mouth and the bowl. He wondered, if they would know that the person behind spoiling their son's game was slurping dahi-vade in front of them, it definitely would drive them crazy. Gourav put his bowl down on the side table and emptied the glass of water in one take.

Gourav shuffled restlessly on his seat. "I am done Mami. Sorry, but I'll finish all these the next time maybe. I will quickly meet Vivek and leave," Gourav said and went to Vivek's room. Vivek was combing his hair and shaping up spikes in front of the mirror. He saw Gourav's reflection in the mirror, standing behind him. "Hey bro! When did you come?"

"Hey! It's been some time, was relishing the special dahi-vade made for you."

Vivek smiled. "Here is your share," Gourav showed the white packet to Vivek. Vivek turned to Gourav, hesitating in taking it. "You keep this… you are in need this time. Later you can return it to me, no problem at all," he insisted.

"If I will need it, I will definitely tell you. But right now, these are your earnings and you should take them. And how was your cricket series? I hope no one has any doubt on you?" With that, Gourav placed the packet before him on the table.

"Yeah, no one has, yet."

"Will you play for me in the next series also?"

"What… again?" Vivek asked, surprised.

"Bro, I need money to pay off the bank loan. This is the only way I can earn surplus. And I need you. You will get your share on time. I won't let you compromise."

"But this time it won't be good for my career."

"I also don't want to affect your career. Believe me, in India, people worship cricket and cricket players. Only a few bad performances can't ruin your career. This time, I want you to talk to some other players as well. Maybe Amit Yogi, the spinner; and Sunil Choudhary, the fast bowler. If both are ready to play on our side, I assure you, we could earn tremendous amount of money," Gourav tried to persuade him.

"If they refuse to be a part of this plan, then? Wouldn't everything be disclosed to them also?" Vivek expressed his doubts.

"You will have to be clever when you talk to them. First comprehend their attitude; what is in their heart. Money has the power to attract everyone. So whether they believe in a fair game or the money game, you have to sniff that out. My deal is for thirteen lakh rupees for all of you. And the other thing, I want them in the semi-finals or the finals," Gourav said.

"I'm meeting them in Mumbai next week. I will try speaking to them there."

Gourav gave a new SIM card to Vivek. And gave nick names 'Bull' and 'Bunny' to Amit and Sunil, respectively, for further communication.

An unpredictable game

In Mumbai, Vivek got the opportunity to talk to both the players, and he finally convinced them to play as per Gourav's idea. It was not easy for Vivek; he was an amateur. But Amit Yogi was smart enough to realise Vivek's actual intention behind all that talk. He asked directly if he had any deal for him. Vivek told him about Gourav and his quote. Amit asked for thirteen lakh rupees for each match and assured further that he would talk to Sunil Choudhary regarding that.

Gourav accepted his proposal.

The cricket series started. Nitin and Gourav were busy making strategies according to the bets. Vivek was providing him information about the players, pitch and weather, time to time.

In the tournament, Sri Lanka, India and Pakistan got two points each and reached the semi-finals. Now, the first semi-final was between Sri Lanka and India. Nitin and Gourav didn't find any big bet against which they were willing to manipulate the game, so they left the match alone. India won that match. The second semi-final was between India and Pakistan. In that match, Gourav gave instructions to Vivek to cross sixty runs. India won again and entered the finals. The third semi-final match was between Sri Lanka and Pakistan, which Pakistan won.

Now the final was between India and Pakistan.

The world's eyes are glued to TVs when these two teams play against each other. Excitement could be seen at every nook and corner. Kids were playing cricket wearing Indian cricket team caps. Youngsters were busy discussing the most important issue; 'Who will win the finals?' 'India has the advantage, as it has defeated Pakistan twice, once in league and once in semi-finals. The morale of our players is high.' 'Pakistani players must be annoyed about their past two defeats. It's possible they will play a more aggressive and competitive game in the fit of pique. It's not good to count your chickens before they hatch. What if our players become overconfident? It's too early to make judgments.'

"I have high expectations from this final match," Gourav said. "The wagers were not big in previous matches. But I am sure we will get some large wagers for finals. Our clients must put their money on Indian cricketers for sure."

"We should make a strategy accordingly," Nitin said.

"We will use our other two trump cards in this match, Amit and Sunil."

"Hmm," Nitin pulled a chair and sat down. "For Pakistan to win, it's necessary that the run rate of India does not go high. We can ask Vivek to play slow and safe, be on the pitch for a long time and not let the run rate go beyond five. Amit and Sunil could do easy bowling to which the Pak players could easily hit boundaries, some more wides and no balls," Nitin said.

"I am also thinking to place our wager with other bookies in favour of Pakistan as a punter, what do you say?" Gourav asked Nitin.

"Great, man," his eyes got wider. "We can earn double with this brilliant idea, wow!" Nitin said, excited.

Gourav called up Vivek and told him his strategy.

Nitin was right; some big bets got involved in that match.

The match started. India won the toss and decided to bat first. The stadium was packed. There was little traffic on the roads, most of the nooks and corners of the cities were empty. Everyone wanted to watch that match.

Indian opening batsmen were on the crease. In the very first over, they scored nine runs with two boundaries and one single. The whole country cheered. By the fifth over, India had scored twenty-nine runs; both the batsmen were not missing any opportunity to strike the ball to the boundary.

Gourav's heartbeat was increasing after every boundary. He was praying, 'May god take their wicket.'

"They seem to be in an attacking mood, the run rate is touching six," Nitin said and adjusted himself in his chair. Suddenly, the batsman raised the ball up on mid-off, which could be a catch for the fielder positioned there. The country held its breath for a second. Some were praying to god to make the fielder miss that catch. And the fielder missed the catch finally. The country released its breath and cheered.

"I can't believe it! How could he drop the catch! Pathetic fielding… why don't they improve their fielding and practise catches?" Gourav stamped his fist on the table in disappointment.

"Their partnership could be dangerous if it's not broken soon," Nitin said.

Gourav was sweating profoundly. He was relieved when the umpire declared LBW after the 11th over. Vivek came up for batting; the score was sixty-two runs after the loss of one wicket. For the initial overs, Vivek played defensive and was taking singles. Sometimes he was taking doubles so that the other batsman would get fewer opportunities to bat. Nitin and Gourav were happy when the run rate fell to five. Second wicket fell in the 16th over as a run out. Vivek cleverly made him run out by stopping him in the middle of the crease. Until the batsman reached back to his crease, he was stumped out. Commentators disparaged Vivek's unwise call. After the second wicket fell, the match went slowly, the number of boundaries decreased.

"The team is under pressure. It seems both the batsmen are struggling before Pakistani bowlers. But it is important they play safe, there is no need to get impatient. India needs a stable partnership right now," The commentator stated.

After twenty overs, the score was ninety-one runs with two wickets down, not a desirable run rate at all. The audience was disappointed because no sixes and fours were being hit. In the 25th over, the third wicket fell when the wicket keeper caught a simple catch. A new batsman came and tried to speed up the run rate. In his first over, he hit two boundaries. The audience cheered with the hope that he would do something. Vivek was also hitting fours in between to save his position, but he was trying to get more strikes.

Some cricket lovers wanted Vivek to be out; because of him, the run rate was blocked. They were even disappointed when he made a half century.

"Fifty runs in eighty balls, ridiculous."

Vivek got out in the 39th over. The delivered ball hit the off stump behind him. He had scored sixty-nine runs. The new batsman who came after him tried to make runs faster. At the end of the first innings, India had scored 248 runs with the loss of 7 wickets.

"Two hundred and forty-nine runs could be an easy target for Pakistan to chase. Now, all the responsibility lies on the shoulders of Indian bowlers," the commentators said.

"Vivek couldn't do more than that, he did whatever he could, and we can't expect more from him," Nitin said. "It's not a huge target. Pakistan will chase it easily. Moreover, we also have two bowlers; they will make this target easier for them. We are going to earn lots of money after that, from both the sides, as bookie as well as puntera!" Nitin said in excitement.

"I wish," Gourav said with a smile and ordered a pizza.

The second innings had started. Pakistani batsmen were on the crease.

To the boys' shock and the cheers of cricket lovers, Pakistan's first wicket fell in the very first over.

"What the crap!" Gourav screamed, a bite of pizza falling from his mouth when the wicket keeper caught the ball, and the umpire raised his index finger to declare the batsman out.

"Oh shit!" Nitin also screamed with him. "Out in the first over?" For the next forty seconds, he didn't take his eyes off the TV, and then had a bite of pizza. "Gourav, please pass me the chilli flakes. This match is going to be more interesting, I want to make it spicier. This bloody bookmaking has made us anti-Indian. See, when the entire country is cheering for India, we are here getting blue over this," he said, tongue-in-cheek, and concentrated on the pizza.

After four overs, Amit Yogi came to bowl. As was fixed, he was doing easy bowling, and giving extra runs through wide and no balls. After ten overs, Pakistan's score was 55 for the loss of 1 wicket. In the 12th over, the second wicket fell, which slowed their run rate.

The new batsman was struggling to settle down at the crease. Sunil Choudhary bowled him a full toss, which he hit for a boundary. The ball got flipped in the air towards log on. Vivek was fielding there and he dropped that catch. The whole country must have been cursing him, except the two boys who felt relief after seeing him safe. But their relief was not for long. The sixth ball of the over, Sunil Choudhary again bowled a full toss. The batsman flipped the ball towards extra cover, and this time, the fielder caught the ball without any mistake. Pakistan lost its third wicket in the 16th over. In next three overs, one more wicket fell; the batsman was run out.

The match seemed completely in the Indian team's grasp now.

"What is happening there? What are the Pakistani batsmen doing? They don't have fire or what? Can't they even take on a simple target, bullshit?" Nitin groaned in frustration.

"They can't give up… they can't give up… otherwise, whatever we have done… all ruined," Gourav was cracking his knuckles nervously and murmuring.

Forty-five overs were done and Pakistan's score was 196 with 7 wickets down. Pakistan had little hope; only sixes and fours could do that miracle. It lost its 8th wicket in the 46th over and 9th in the 48th over. Only one wicket was left and the score was 212. The public had already assumed that India had won the match and was celebrating. People were waving the Indian flag in the stadium, kids were out on the roads and the crackle of fireworks could be heard. Very soon, Pakistan lost its 10th wicket also. India won the match by 27 runs.

No end to problems

They lost a huge amount. All the bets they played as punter and all the bets that punters played with them. Nitin and Gourav were bound to pay everyone, their punters, their bookies and also to the players. They lost everything they had won from the cricket series. To repay his load, Gourav sold his ancestral land with a heavy heart.

He had just repaid his dues, when he received a bank notice. The legal department had declared his shop NPA, i.e. Non-Performing Asset. Through Securitisation and Reconstruction of Financial Assets and Enforcement of Security Interest Act, 2002 (SARFAESI), the bank had seized the shop. Gourav didn't have any hope of reclaiming his property; he was completely in the red.

His father was totally shattered. They had no means of living left, neither his business nor his son's. Gourav was finding it difficult to face him. From where would he manage money for his mother's treatment now?

Gourav, Rajeev and Nitin were sitting in a park. Gourav lamented, "I lost everything." His eyes filled with pain and tears.

Rajeev tried to console him. "Don't lose hope. Just take it as a bad phase of life. Everyone has to pass through it once in life. And you are passing through it."

Nitin said in a low voice. "Ya, we went through a bad time. Can you believe it, Rajeev? We earned like never before, and it all slipped through our fingers suddenly! I cannot believe it yet… damn!" He held open his bare palm.

"I still can't get how Pak lost the match. It was an easy match for them to win," Rajeev asked.

They were silent for a few seconds.

"It was a fixed match on their side," Gourav broke the silence with his low voice.

Rajeev's eyes widened in shock. He yelled, "Is it? What are you saying?"

Gourav spoke again in the same low voice. "We crassly tried to manipulate the game. We were too dumb to realise that we were taking a high risk. Pakistan's team is rife with fixing." He was exasperated. "How could we be so foolish? Papa had told me once, 'be alert, an alert mind can avert the danger', but I repeated the same mistake."

In the meantime, Nitin's mobile rang; it was Mr Ajeez on the other side. He wanted to meet them at 4.30 p.m. the next day at his hotel.

"Tomorrow we are going to meet him, but never let our connection with Vivek and the others slip out to him. The whole thing should be confidential," Nitin said.

"I won't be able to come with you guys," Rajeev told them. "I was about to tell you. I got a promotion and they are transferring me to their Mumbai branch. I have to leave for Mumbai tomorrow, I have a meeting there."

"Congratulations, dear," Gourav said, suppressing his grief, and patted Rajeev's shoulder.

"Yeah, man, congrats! It's great. So when are you joining there?" Nitin asked.

"It will be decided in the coming few days," Rajeev said.

"Okay, so like Amit, you are also going far, haan," Nitin said woefully.

"Come on, don't say these things. We are friends, and we will always be friends. The thing that is bothering me is, I am leaving my friends in their critical time. I wish I could be with you." Rajeev came close to Nitin and Gourav and hugged them both.

"It's fine. Don't worry, focus on your future, buddy. It's also not easy for you; we know that. You have to settle down in an unknown city. But we are very happy for you. You come back from Mumbai and we will celebrate," Gourav said.

Next day, in the hotel, Mr Ajeez was sitting in the coffee shop, reading a newspaper when Gourav and Nitin entered the place, and after greeting him, they sat down.

"For how many days are you in the city?" Nitin asked.

"Just for three days. Tomorrow, I will be leaving for Bangladesh." He ordered some snacks and hot coffee. After a pause, he asked, "How was the bookmaking business in the Asia cup matches?"

"Sir, we faced a huge loss in this series, like never before. I even lost my shop," Gourav said.

"Lost your shop, how come?" Mr Ajeez asked in shock.

Gourav told him about the infamous poisonous drug scandal and the bank notice.

Ajeez said, "Ahh, that's really bad. I'll give you some advice. It's risky to run bookmaking independently when big bets are involved. You have already tasted that experience, haven't you?"

"Ya, we have had enough," Gourav mourned.

"If you are getting big wagers, then it's better for you to join a syndicate. It's a huge chain of bookmakers. Every bookie is connected through each other in the system and gets a safety net of the syndicate if their losses get too high."

Gourav said, "Oh yes, I have heard about this, but don't know how it functions."

The waiter brought coffee and snacks and placed them on the table.

Ajeez picked up some fries and said, "I know someone personally who can help you in this. Naseef Ali is a big bookie in Delhi. He was in the US for the past six months, and just returned. You can meet him, give my reference. But he doesn't take everyone's call, so call him by 9 o'clock. Before that, I will speak to him about you," Ajeez said and gave them Naseef's number.

At 9, they called up Naseef Ali and fixed a meeting with him for the next day.

A well-organised business

Nitin and Gourav were sitting in the café when a tall, wheatish-complexioned man around 6 feet in height, of middle age, came towards them. He wore a blue shirt with white collar and cuffs, black pants with matching black shoes. He came near and asked, "Aaaa, Mr Nitin?"

"Yes, yes," Nitin said and stood up.

"I am Naseef." He shook hands with both and sat. "Ajeez told me you run your own bookmaking business."

"Yes, for almost a year. We want to join the syndicate," Nitin said.

Naseef explained to them what the syndicate in bookmaking was and how it functioned.

Syndicate is the top position in the betting business. It is followed by first-tier bookies, then second- and third-tier bookies and so on, and at last the customers. The ranking was based upon the number of customers they had.

Naseef was a two-tier bookie and had more than one hundred fifty customers.

He asked them to communicate with each other through Blackberry messenger. He also gave them a website address, where they could get odds from the syndicate. A betting syndicate is a group that takes bets from all over India. They decide what the betting odds should be, they open up their prices and customers bet on their prices. There are only four main betting markets run across the country – the match odds, lambi, brackets, and Lunch favourite. Among all, "match odds" are most popular, in which the punter has to decide whether the price fixed by the syndicate is good and decide to back a team to win or lose.

"Bracket" is also known as session betting. It's available when the match is underway and updated ball-by-ball. A batting team would be given a runs spread for a ten-over segment on how many runs would be scored in that segment. And customers would decide whether to bet over or under that run spread at odds. It's most popular in ODI and T-20 matches.

"Lambi" is the term used for innings runs. At the start of an inning, the betting team will be given a runs spread, and customers decide whether to bet over or under that run spread. It is also updated ball-by-ball.

"Lunch Favourite" is offered as a forward bet, or pre-match bet. It is available in Test match and ODI. A customer bets on selecting a pre-determined price for whichever team is considered the favourite at the innings break in ODI or lunch break in a Test match.

"I hope you guys are clear on using *bhao line*, money transfer through *hawala* and all," Naseef said.

They shook their heads. "We have heard about it, but never applied it in our practice," Gourav said.

"Okay, I'll take you to my office, you guys will have a better idea then," Naseef said.

Naseef drove them to Patel Nagar where his office was. The car entered a narrow lane with dilapidated buildings. At the end of the lane, the car stopped in front of a curious ramshackle house.

They got down from the car. Nitin and Gourav looked at the three-storey house. It hadn't been white washed for ages. Some grey patches of paint could be seen on some parts of the building, otherwise bare bricks eagerly peeped out from the wall plaster. A tiny Peepal shrub had somehow managed to grow between the cracks of the house. They wondered if the house would crumble in an earthquake.

Naseef figured out what they were thinking. He said, "We are in an illegal business, and this place is quite safe from the police's eye. Posh areas are not recommended for bookmaking. The building has a firm foundation, so don't worry."

They reached the third floor. Naseef knocked, and a young man opened the door. Naseef took them inside. It looked like a living room. Naseef took them into an adjoining room. There was a man sitting on the bed with his legs crossed; he tried to stand up as they entered. Naseef signalled him to sit down and carry on with his work. He sat, held his mobile in one hand and put the ear phone on. He was speaking continually on his phone.

"He is the *bhao line* operator. The syndicate provides odds and these operators continuously read out the live match odds over the telephone line, where customers can hear them and place their wagers," Naseef said.

The man who opened the door came and took his seat next to him and started recording bets. He opened a laptop and input some data. Naseef asked Gourav and Nitin to watch him work. Then he showed them the software through which each and every bet was recorded. He showed them bookies' records. Bookies used to pass a percentage of their bets on to other bookies. If he keeps all his bets, the amounts will be too high, whether profit or loss.

Naseef taught them how to use the software and its various options. "If you will click this, it will show you the profits and loss for individual customers and bookies. And here I'm showing you the spreadsheet of how much money the syndicate is making state by state. Here is Punjab, Delhi, Uttar Pradesh, Maharashtra, and so on. You can see this is a well-organised business."

"How many offices like this do you have, Naseef?" Nitin asked.

"In Delhi, I have three centres, two in Punjab and one in Haryana. Each centre has two persons for recording and writing down the wagers next to the name of the customer. One more thing, never use the original names of customers, and use nicknames like 'M-Rock' or 'Tiger'. Each bet is struck via a cell phone, as you can see. Everything is recorded, so there can be no dispute. Each customer has a credit account. If a customer is new, we prefer to take cash in advance, and once he is trusted, we provide him a credit account. Customers are paid the next day of a match, through hawala system. Here, the money is transferred through a network of hawala brokers. A customer approaches a hawala broker in one city and gives a sum of money to transfer to a recipient in another city. All parties are given a code or password. And for each transaction, a customer has to pay a small sum of money to the bookie. And this is how the bookmaking industry functions," Naseef said.

Both Nitin and Gourav asked some questions to clear their doubts, then thanked Naseef and took his leave.

On their way home, Nitin asked Gourav, "Do you think it is safe?"

"I hope so. It's a well-organised network, everyone is connected, and the risk is very low. We should take a chance, maybe this time luck will favour us," Gourav said.

After that, Gourav was giving plenty of time to the business and gaining expertise. He met Nassef and the other bookies regularly to build a good rapport in the industry.

Goa

Gourav was at the Delhi airport, going to Goa to meet Vivek, to talk about a match series, which was to be held after a month. During security check-in, a security person asked, "Whose bag is this?"

Gourav saw that the security person held a black bag. "It is mine sir, is there any problem?" he asked.

"Yes, we need to check this," the security person yelled.

"But it has only a few clothes and papers inside," Gourav said and adjusted the code lock. The bag didn't open.

The security person looked at him suspiciously. Gourav tried again with a different code, but in vain.

"You don't remember your code?" The security person asked, raising an eyebrow.

"I don't know what happened. I do remember my lock's code. I can't say what went wrong," Gourav said shocked.

The security person called some staff and ordered them to cut the lock. Gourav stood by, looking helpless. The bag was opened.

Gourav yelled in shock. "It is not mine."

The security person stared at Gourav. "My bag looks just like that, but it's not mine. I... I swear." Gourav swore, keeping his finger on his throat.

The bag was full of ladies' stuff – a make-up kit, a girl's tops and trousers. "Sir, it is my bag." Gourav and the security person both turned their heads in the direction of the voice, there was a girl claiming her bag.

"Are you sure it is yours, because we need to check it," the security person said.

"Yes, it is mine only. It might be because of the belt, it has a metal buckle," she said.

In between, Gourav excused himself and collected his own black bag and headed for boarding. He was a little embarrassed because of the entire incident.

To his surprise, the same girl came and sat next to him on the plane, and kept the black bag in the luggage rack. Gourav gave her a smile. She smiled back.

"I am really sorry. Because of me, all the confusion was created and your bag got damaged as well," Gourav said.

"It's okay… no apology, please," she said.

"But this time, I will be careful," Gourav said.

She looked at him with suspicion. "What do you mean?"

"Both our bags are together in the compartment. And I think we can't bear the cost of confusion this time because of the exchange of our bags," Gourav said.

She was laughing her head off at his joke. Her laugh made Gourav also laugh with her.

"You are right; we have to be more careful…ha…ha!" She held her breath for a while. "Imagine, I get yours and you get my bag …ha… ha…!" She paused to catch her breath and continued, "…What will happen…" She gave a deep rumbling laugh at her own joke.

Gourav also chuckled to see her laughing. Her eyes were bright and wet because of all the laughter. The way she was catching her breath between laughs, ruffling her hair from time to time, and her sparkling pink lips captivated Gourav. In the last few months, Gourav had hardly felt any kind of felicity or pleasure. And after a long time, in her presence, he felt a kind of relaxation… like life was beautiful. Stuck with the daily chaos of life, we forget that life is also to enjoy, to feel lively, and to admire nature's beauty.

"Do you have relatives in Goa?" she asked after the laughter session.

Her voice broke the spell and Gourav took his eyes off her face. "I am going there for business," he said and buckled his safety belt as the plane was ready to take off.

"I am going there to spend my holidays with my friends. They have already reached there one day in advance. I had to submit my project today, so I submitted and rushed to the airport. By the way, I am Shalini. I am doing PG in Geography."

"My name is Gourav."

"What business do you do?"

"Aaaah… it's related to sports," Gourav said and wondered at how difficult it was to describe his work to someone.

"Great… nice meeting you." She smiled and took out a magazine from her hand-bag. Gourav glanced at it; it was *Stardust.* Gourav preferred to take a nap, and stretched out on his seat till they reached Goa.

❖

Gourav reached the hotel where Vivek was staying with his friends. Vivek introduced him to his friends. Gourav had a fun time with them, during which he almost forgot the past few months. They hired bikes and hung out on the streets of Goa, with great food and wine. It has a totally different culture, which spreads magic in the air.

In the evening, they reached Tito's, a famous dance club in Goa. Loud music, sparkling laser lights, beverage counter, hundreds of boys and girls dancing on the floor. Vivek and his friends joined the crowd. Gourav tried to adjust his eyes to the dazzling lights, when he saw a familiar girl in a tube top.

Gourav recognised Shalini. He went to say hello to her.

"Hey… Hi… you are here… what a coincidence," she said loudly in his ear as the music was very loud.

"I came with my friends," he said loudly.

"Meet my friends." She introduced him to her friends. "Hey girls, he is Gourav, we met in the flight. And Gourav, she is Kirti… Pooja… and she is Garima."

Gourav also called his friends and introduced them to Shalini and her friends. "He is Vivek…" He was interrupted as they recognised Vivek.

"Oooh… he is Vivek! Who the hell doesn't know him? He is a star cricketer…" The girls screamed in excitement and shook hands with him.

Gourav continued when they were through with Vivek. "He is Sumit, he is Rajnish, and he is Varun."

After the inclusion of the girls, the party got spicier for the boys… dance and fun all night. Rajnish and Sumit asked the girls if they would like to have some more vodka. Obviously, the night was long and to last on the dance floor over-night, that was needed.

Vivek announced that they would be going to Baga beach the next morning and asked the girls to come, to which they agreed. Shalini exchanged her mobile number with Gourav for further communication. The DJ was playing peppy numbers, and on the dance floor, Gourav had become close to Shalini. Her eyes were looking brighter in the dazzling lights, her dark hair was rippling left-right on her every movement, and moreover, in an orange tube top, she was looking very sexy. Everyone toasted for Goa and gulped their tequila shots. Gourav started getting tipsy. He looked around for Shalini. "Where is Shalini?" he asked Kriti.

"She went outside... she'll come in some time," Kirti said, pointing out the entrance.

Gourav went outside to look for her. She was sitting on the sofa chair. "Are you okay?" he asked.

"Yeah... I am fine," she said and sat straight on the sofa.

"Sure?" he asked again.

"I tasted tequila for the first time... so just a little bit... by the way, what are you doing here?" she diverted the conversation.

"I didn't see you inside, so I came looking for you. You know, it was my first time too... and now I am feeling out of the world." He came and sat near Shalini.

"Do you believe in destiny, Gourav?" she asked.

"Yes, I do, because what is happening to me for the last few months, only destiny could do that," Gourav said.

"Isn't it strange, we met first at the airport, and then our seats were together in the flight, and now here? We are also going to meet tomorrow. It can't be just a coincidence."

Gourav looked in her eyes and asked softly, "Then what is it?"

She met his eyes and said, "It's destiny. We are meeting again and again because our destiny wants it."

Whether it was the tequila or the effect of the intoxicating environment, they came closer. The sound of music filtered out, couples were hovering around. Some had come outside to smoke and others had come to chill in the open air. For the time being, Gourav forgot the mischief of his destiny and thanked it for bringing sweetness to his life. He brought his face closer. Her magnificent aroma delighted him; he wanted to kiss her glossy orange lips. Shalini's eyes were set on Gourav, she sensed what he wanted. She slowly closed her eyes and allowed him to kiss her. As their lips met, a strong sensation passed through their bodies. They might have experienced that for a long time if their friends hadn't interrupted them.

"See, we came to look if everything is fine with her, and here she is with Gourav," Garima emphasised his name and giggled.

The spell was broken. Gourav and Shalini quickly moved apart. Shalini felt embarrassed in front of her friends. Kirti elbowed her to tease her and raised her eyebrows. Shalini blushed and told her friend, "Let's go inside." She held Kirti's hand and turned towards the door. While getting in, she looked back, and Gourav gave her a smile. He was wondering what had just happened; he could still feel the warmth of her lips on his.

He lit a cigarette and puffed some smoke in the air, thinking about her. "Was it just an infatuation or something else? Does she have feelings for me or what? And more importantly, what do I feel for her? Yeah, I like the way she laughs, I like looking at her black bright eyes. When I didn't see her inside, I was eager to check whether she was okay or not, and I came outside to see her. So do I care for her? Yes, I want to know more about her. Yes, I admire her. And yes, I am happy that we are meeting again tomorrow. I am falling in love."

It was a nice sunny day in Goa. A cool breeze was ruffling the surface of the sea. The boys were enjoying their day to the fullest. After enjoying a few water rides, the girls also arrived, looking stunning in their beach dresses. But Shalini caught Gourav's eye. She had worn pink shorts with an over sized white shirt, through which her matching pink bra could be seen. She had put on a wide-brimmed hat and sunglasses to protect her from the bright sunlight.

Gourav couldn't help but tell her, "You are looking… stunning." He wanted to say hot, but he changed the word.

"Thanks," she said happily.

Vivek announced for everyone to play beach volleyball.

"Yeah!" everyone screamed.

The group had been divided into girls' v/s boys'. They played for an hour. When everyone got tired, they spread a large mat on the sand and sat, relaxing in the cool sea breeze. Gourav, Rajnish, Kirti and Garima went to get some cold drinks and snacks. It was the time when they came to know more about each other, they were talking, cracking jokes, pulling each other's legs. "Now we should go inside the water," Rajnish said.

"Yeah, let's go now," the others also said.

"I will be here only," Shalini said.

"Hey, come on, it will be fun," Kirti said and pulled her up.

"No, no, no, I'm scared of the sea." Shalini requested them to leave her.

"Kirti is right. What is the use of coming here and not playing in the sea? Come with us… it is a wonderful experience," Pooja said.

Shalini stood up after they insisted, and went with them in the water. Little waves were chasing each other to the sea shore and breaking down. They were playing and enjoying getting wet. Suddenly, a high wave knocked Shalini off her balance. She fell, and floated away. Gourav and Varun saw her floating; they dived in no time and saved her after some struggle.

All of them came out of the water. She was coughing badly; the salty water had gone inside her throat and nose. She was shivering with fear and cold, and started crying. Everyone was busy consoling her.

In between, Gourav went and brought a shirt from his bag. Shalini wore the shirt and expressed a desire to go back to the hotel. Gourav took the bike's key from Vivek and went to drop her to the hotel. Shalini sat behind and placed her hand on Gourav's shoulder. A strong sensation ran through him. No girl had ever sat behind him on his bike. He was a little conscious; he kept asking her if she was fine.

They reached the hotel. Shalini insisted Gourav come inside and have some tea. Shalini's room was on the fourth floor, so they took the lift. Shalini had been very quiet, but now she broke her silence. "Thanks, you saved my life."

"Mention not. I just did my duty," he said.

"But I mean it. You don't know how scared I am of the sea. I am feeling like I had a brush with death." A horrified expression appeared on her face.

Gourav embraced her to relax her. "Oh forget it. Now everything is fine."

Lift reached the fourth floor, and they stepped out. Shalini unlocked the door and went in. "I am sharing this room with Kirti. Sorry, it's a little messy," she said.

The dressing table was full of accessories. The coffee table near the window was loaded with the dresses that the girls had worn last night. Sandals were lined up in the corner of the room. A blanket was spread over the bed, the pillows in disarray.

'Hmm, so this is what a girl's room looks like,' Gourav said to himself.

"Oh… it's so embarrassing. Actually, yesterday we came late and we didn't have the energy to keep stuff back in place. And again in the morning, we left for the beach in a hurry. Everything is scattered, sheesh!" Shalini kept talking while arranging her room. She removed the clothes from the chair and put them in the wardrobe. "Please, have a seat," she told Gourav as she arranged the bed.

"What would you like to have, tea or coffee?" she asked.

"Coffee."

"Fine. Just dial room service and order it. Till then I can take a shower and come," she said and got into the bathroom.

Gourav ordered two coffees. It was a strange feeling to be in a girl's room when the girl was taking a shower and he was ordering coffee on the phone. His inner voice said that he was in the room of the girl he loves and what he wanted to know was whether she loved him or not. He looked around, the room was filled with the same aroma which he had smelled last night when he was with Shalini.

The doorbell rang, and the waiter brought coffee on a tray. Gourav took the tray from him and closed the door. Shalini came out from the bathroom. She wore a blue gown and was drying her hair with a towel.

"Madam, your coffee is ready," Gourav said and smiled.

Shalini smiled and sat on another chair in front of Gourav and picked up the kettle to prepare coffee. Gourav kept looking at her. She looked fresh and pure after a bath, not a single mark of makeup, her hair wet and falling over her face. The dark blue gown made her look fairer and prettier. Her eyes met his, when she handed him the coffee mug.

"What?" she asked.

"Ah, nothing." Gourav looked down and took the coffee mug from her. "You look different, prettier," he said.

"Thanks," she said and blushed.

"How are you feeling now?" he asked and sipped his coffee.

"Much better. I have recovered from the shock. Terrible experience, I must say," she said and sipped her coffee.

"I also got scared seeing you in that situation." Shalini looked at Gourav, as he continued, "I would confess that my heart was beating crazily, as though something dear to me was slipping from my grip."

Silence descended for a while. And finally, Gourav asked her, "Shalini, last night, whatever happened between us, what does that mean for you?"

Shalini placed her coffee mug on the table and adjusted herself on the chair like she was preparing herself to confess. "It was a beautiful moment for me, which I would like to cherish for long." Gourav's heart filled with delight on hearing those words from her. She continued, "You know, I strongly believe in destiny. The day I met you, I felt some attraction towards you, and see, we met again and again. I feel a kind of comfort in your company. I am sitting with you in this room just because I feel you are the right person for me."

Gourav could see the reflection of her truth and emotion in her eyes. He stood up and went to hug her. He kissed her forehead. He cupped her face, looked into her eyes and said, "I love you… and I mean it."

"I love you too," Shalini replied.

Gourav kissed her, again, and this time, it was deeper and more intense. They kissed again and again passionately. Gourav slid the straps of her gown and kissed her bare shoulder. She slipped away from his grip and turned away with sensations. Gourav softly slid her wet hair away and kissed her nape. He discovered that the gown had a zip at the back, and he slowly unzipped it. Shalini turned back and hugged him tight. Gourav's hands were running on her back, and finally, he succeeded in unhooking her bra. Her body was still cold and he could smell her soap. He took her in his lap and carefully put her on the bed, bending over to kiss her. Shalini stretched her arm and switched off the lights. Both cuddled inside the blanket and made love.

They were lying under the blanket, their clothes spread beside the bed. Gourav was looking at the ceiling. Shalini was lying near him, and her hand was resting on his chest.

"What are you thinking?" she asked.

"Nothing," he said, still looking at the ceiling.

"I am feeling so light and complete with you."

He smiled and kissed her forehead. "Me too, love you," he said. "I am leaving for Delhi tomorrow."

"When is your flight?"

"8:45 in morning."

"I will be back day after tomorrow. We will go on a date then," she said. "You will have to spare some time for me from your busy schedule. By the way, what kind of sports business do you do?"

"Yeah, you should know everything about me. That day in the flight, I told you that I am into the sports business, but it is of a different kind. I am in the bookmaking business. But my dream is to open my own shop." And Gourav told her everything related to his family and business, all the ups and down of his life. Shalini listened to him carefully.

"Now I have told you everything, my life is an open book for you. You tell me about yourself."

"My life is not as complicated as yours. My father is in the Navy, and most of the time, he travels across different countries. I lost my mother when I was only seven. My grandparents brought me up. Since then, I have been living with them. My father comes home once or twice in a year, but I am more attached to my grandma, she is like a friend. After the current course, I want to go to Mumbai to do an interior designing course. I hope grandpa will agree and allow me, otherwise I have my magic stick, my grandma, she hardly says no to me." She was interrupted by a phone call from Kirti.

"How are you now? Are you okay?" Kirti asked.

"Yes, I am all right."

"By the way, is Gourav still with you?" Shalini looked at Gourav and wasn't able to decide what to say to her. "Hmm, your silence is telling us the whole story. You guys are together, right? Yesterday we noticed something was going on between you, isn't it?" Shalini blushed as her secret was discovered. "By the way, I called you up to tell you that Vivek is asking us to come to Royal Casino this evening. What do you say? Would you like to go there? If you are not feeling okay, then we won't go," she said.

"I am fine now. We will go there," Shalini said.

"Okay. We are also leaving for the hotel," she said and hung up.

"You didn't tell me that you were going to the casino today," Shalini queried.

"Yeah, my friends were planning something like that… it skipped my mind. So you are also coming?" Gourav said.

"Hmm… Now turn around and close your eyes," she collected her clothes and said.

"What's the need?" Gourav said. Shalini threw a pillow on his face. "Okay, my eyes are closed… you can."

"No, you could cheat, just turn," she said and lovingly pushed him. "The girls could come any time. Hey, don't turn, I am not done yet," she screamed when Gourav tried to turn.

On thinking a bit more on it, Shalini told Gourav, "You should leave now."

"You are a very mean person," Gourav complained.

"What? Would it look nice if they discover you inside the blanket like this?" she argued.

"But I can't leave without my clothes. Let me put on my clothes. How can I, if you stand in front of me like this?" he said.

"Yeah, yeah, you put your clothes on. Till then, I will go to the bathroom and freshen up," she said and turned towards the bathroom.

"And don't try to cheat," Gourav teased her.

Gourav and Vivek were sitting in their hotel, talking about the upcoming cricket tournament. Gourav gave him a new SIM card and asked him to keep updating him.

The group went to Royal casino that evening, which was on a ship. There, they enjoyed gambling. The upper floor had a banquet. They had dinner together and left for their hotels.

Next morning, Gourav flew back to Delhi.

The call of destiny

In Delhi, Shalini and Gourav dated each other for a while. Finally, he proposed marriage and took her home one day to let her meet his parents.

Gourav's mother was very happy to see such a beautiful and lovely bride for her son. She wanted to hug her, but her illness stopped her from doing that. She just blessed her for bringing happiness in Gourav's life. Shalini had won the hearts of Gourav's parents. His father promised her that soon he would come to her place to talk to her grandparents.

Gourav and his father reached Shalini's home. She lived with her grandparents in a flat in Hauz Khas. Gourav rang the bell. An old lady opened the door; Gourav sensed that she was Shalini's grandma.

"Namaste, I am Gourav. Shalini might have told you about me," he joined his hands and introduced himself.

"Yes, yes, come. She is my granddaughter," she said softly and greeted them. Gourav's father also said namaste to her.

"Please be seated. I will call her grandpa," she said and went inside.

Shalini's grandpa entered. Gourav and his father stood up and they exchanged greetings. He signalled them to sit down.

“I met Shalini. She had come home last week. She is a lovely girl. I am sure you know, that our children like each other,” his father said.

“My wife told me everything. Shalini is the apple of our eye, we never say no to her. Her mother passed away ages ago, and her father comes home for a very short time each year. So we always try to fulfil her desires as much as we can. She shouldn’t feel the absence of her parents. But marriage is a different thing, it’s a matter of her life, and we would like to take her father’s consent too.” He paused as Shalini brought some snacks and tea for all. “What do you do, Gourav?” her grandpa asked.

That was the question he hated the most. “I am in a business,” he kept the answer short.

Her grandpa was looking at him, expecting more details of his business. Gourav’s father understood. He said, “Actually, Gourav was working at a pharmaceutical company before, but he always wanted to start his own business, maybe because from childhood, he had seen his father and uncle as businessmen. He left his job and opened his own pharmacy. Everything was going well, but due to his mother’s illness, I had to shut my business, because it became unmanageable after some time. All the pressure came upon him. Unfortunately, we faced hard financial times, and he was unable to make his EMI payments for his shop. The bank seized his shop.” He took a deep breath and continued, “Right now, he and his friends are running a small bookmaking business. When he would collect enough funds, he could start his business again.”

“Hmm, I heard that there is lots of money in bookmaking. But it’s illegal, right?” her grandpa asked and sipped his tea.

This time, Gourav spoke up, "Yes, it's illegal in our country, but I don't find it bad. People place bets and we just channelize them. And I am doing it just because I have to do something for my living. Once I have sufficient funds, I'll start my shop once again."

"But as a parent, I would like to see her well settled in life. You are already unsettled in your life, how will she get stability with you?" he said and kept his empty cup on the table.

His words pinched Gourav's heart. It was the bitter truth. He loved her so much, how he wished he could open his heart and show her grandpa that no one could love and care for his granddaughter as much as he could. He placed his tea cup back on the table, which was only half done.

Shalini gave her grandpa a disappointed look and said in irritation, "Dadaji, I beg to disagree with you. Gourav has seen bad times in life, but he is trying to overcome them. What is the surety that I'll never face problems in life. Could you predict that I'll always be happy with someone else, other than Gourav? We also have seen bad days dadaji, haven't we? I hardly remember my mother's face and her love, papa has never been there whenever I needed him, and my days have passed without their love and affection. I never showed you my grief because I never wanted to make you feel low, but it doesn't mean that I never felt their absence in my life." She paused as she realised that she had spoken exceptionally, something that she never wanted to utter in front of them. Her grandmother's eyes became moist. A deep silence covered the room. Shalini closed her eyes as she felt she had made a mistake. Gourav and his father felt a little awkward in the situation.

Shalini tried to gather her thoughts and said softly, "I am sorry, I shouldn't have said all that. Dadaji and dadiji, your love matters a lot to me. I thank god that he has blessed me with your love and affection. I feel the same for Gourav also. I feel very comfortable and blessed with him. He is a very nice and kind person. I met his mother; she is also very nice and caring. I never got a chance to take care of my mother, but now I really want to care for Gourav's mother with all my heart. Dadaji, they are very good people by heart. I would be happy if you support and encourage Gourav rather than to question him." She looked at him hopefully.

Shalini's words had a great impact on everyone in the room. Gourav felt glad listening to her concern for him and his family.

He wanted to assure her grandpa, so he told him, "Dadaji I promise you, I will open my own shop very soon. I also want to settle well in life. And for that, I need your blessings."

His father also said, "The children have chosen each other. Their happiness should be our happiness, what else could we wish for?"

"Well said, this is the only point. But let me talk to my son also. He is Shalini's father; his consent is also needed. Leave everything on god; his wish is our command. Everything is in his hand," Grandpa pointed at a picture of Lord Shiva, joined both hands on his forehead and bowed. "We can't do anything against his wish." Devotees always leave the complex things upon the almighty.

Gourav and his father asked for permission to leave, and came out.

Throughout the way, grandpa's voice was echoing in Gourav's head. "Everything is in god's hands; we can't do anything against his wish." Though he never remembered god even in his bad days, today he wished to ring the temple bells until god took a decision in his favour. He dropped his father home and rushed to the nearby Shiva temple. He spent almost an hour to please god.

Next day, grandpa called up Gourav's father and told him that Shalini's father had given his approval for the marriage.

"It's really very good news," Gourav's father said happily.

"Yes, for him, Shalini's wish matters most of all. If she likes him, then he has no problem with anything else. Now we have to fix the marriage date," grandpa said.

"Sure, I will share this good news with Gourav and his mother; they will be very happy. And I will come to your place to decide how we have to proceed," he said.

Gourav was standing right behind him. He was on cloud nine on hearing this. His belief in god and destiny became even sturdier now.

'There is more to it than meets the eye'

There was a test match series going on in Edgbaston, England, between England, New Zealand and India.

Pushkar Mehta, the head of the syndicate, was sitting in his Dubai residence watching the cricket match between India and New Zealand. Deepak Chopra, a Bollywood actor, was also sitting along with him, watching the match.

Pushkar Mehta had somehow arranged for a webcam at the venue. With this, he could get faster updates compared to the sponsors who take telecast rights, and could change the odds accordingly on the betting website. For this, he had bribed someone in ECB (England and Wales cricket board, the governing body of cricket in England and Wales).

New Zealand's team was batting first. An Indian bowler had bowled three consecutive no balls. A broad smile came on Mehta's face. Mehta had good connections with the cricket world, and with that, he used to fix matches. In that tournament, he had a deal with two Indian bowlers that those bowlers would bowl in favour of New Zealand. For this, each was paid forty-five lakh rupees. At the end of an innings, New Zealand had scored 224 runs for the loss of two wickets.

The second inning started. Indian batsmen were on the crease. India lost two wickets and scored 202 runs. Vivek came as a fifth wicket to play. He scored 40 runs. Despite everyone's expectations that he would score a half century, he gave an easy catch to a mid fielder.

Mehta had been noticing Vivek from the last few months. He surmised, "I think he is playing for someone; his game is manipulated."

"Who could be behind this fixing?" Deepak asked.

"Aahh, it's too early to say, but I am sure it's not his real game, it is fixed," he said and lit his cigar. "This boy is purchasable, I guarantee," he emphasised his each word. "I also have connections and will get him one day, for sure. Everyone needs more money. Just wait and watch, someday he will play for me," Pushkar said and grinned.

He picked up his phone and called someone, giving instructions to that person to get close to Vivek Mishra, and to try and fix a meeting with him.

Satish Kaushik, a first-tier bookie, had more than four hundred customers. He was involved in real estate also. Satish was close to Pushkar, and was helping him in match-fixing.

He used to maintain good contacts with cricketers, their close friends, ex-players, and umpires. According to him, it was easy to befriend English players, because far away from their motherland and family, they felt lonely and bored, and liked making some local friends, who informed them about the new place and spent some time with them. And bookies like him took advantage of their vulnerability. They flattered them, gave them expensive gifts, and pretended to be their well-wishers. And this Satish Kaushik was an expert in the art of persuasion.

Mehta's call gave him food for thought. He had to find some link to reach Vivek. He started calling people to know if anyone had Vivek's number or if someone knew him well. After calling almost ten people, he called up a photographer named Shekhar Dhanraj.

Dhanraj shot for the Indian team, and visited almost all the places where the team went. Satish knew him since last year.

Vivek had contacted Dhanraj for photo shoots and apart from that, he had personally met Vivek 2-3 times. Satish requested him to introduce him to Vivek, as he was a big fan, to which Dhanraj happily agreed.

A few weeks later, Satish received a call from Dhanraj. There was to be a party in Hotel Wellington Inn on Sunday, where he could meet Vivek. He came to the party. He found some of known faces around. He kept greeting them and talking. He met Dhanraj and was with him for the rest of the party. Dhanraj introduced him to some other people also. Later on, Vivek arrived, and was busy meeting people.

"We will wait till he gets free," Dhanraj told Satish. When Vivek went to the bar, Dhanraj asked Satish to come along with him.

He said hello to Vivek and introduced Satish to him as a businessman who was his great fan and had specially come to meet him. Vivek shook hands with Satish. Satish pretended to be in awe while talking to Vivek, and handed over a gift, "This is from my family. My son and my wife are great fans. They bought this for you and packed it, and asked me to get your autograph for them."

Vivek hesitated. "I don't take gifts from my fans. I could give you my autograph, though."

"I understand, but they will be really very happy if you accept this. It's a very small gift; I hope you will like it." Satish insisted.

Vivek enfeebled at his humble entreaty, "Okay, I will, but what's inside?" Vivek asked.

"Look for yourself, it's yours only," Satish said.

Vivek unpacked the gift; there was an expensive Chopard wrist watch glittering inside that dazzled Vivek's and Dhanraj's eyes for a while.

'Why would anyone give such an expensive gift at the very first meeting?' Vivek thought. 'Is there any motive behind this? It's clear that he is making up stories, it could not be his family's choice.'

"Thanks for this beautiful gift, but I can't take this," Vivek said politely.

"We thought it suits your personality," Satish went on with the flattery.

Vivek signed an autograph and gave it to Satish. "Only giving autograph suits us. It's really a pleasure meeting you, Mr Kaushik," he said and shook hands with Satish and Dhanraj and moved away. He started talking to other people. His unpredictable behaviour left Satish standing there, holding his expensive gift.

Satish left the party, came outside the hotel, and called up Pushkar.

"Our plan didn't work," he told him the entire episode. "I can't believe it. He doesn't look that honest. No worries, if not this way, then another way. One day we will get him," Pushkar said.

Friend's wedding

Gourav and Shalini were to be married on 15 November 2010. I was joyful to hear about it, and was making plans to come to India. It had been almost one-and-a-half years since I moved to Germany. I had missed Nitin's marriage, because I had just gone to Germany. So, this time, Richa and I reached India. We were visiting Delhi for the first time after our marriage. The city had become younger and prettier in those days. Delhi had hosted the Commonwealth Games in October 2010, and it had made the city shine.

Gourav's house had been in a transport of joy. The groom was surrounded by his relatives, and the marriage rituals were going on. Nitin and Neha welcomed us with a warm hug. Neha held Richa's hand and went to sit with the women; obviously the sisters had plenty of gossip to share. It was the *haldi* ceremony. Gourav's mother came in a wheelchair to put some haldi on him. Her disease had made her weak and thin. She had covered herself with a blue Pashmina shawl. We went to her and touched her feet. She looked very happy. Till then, Rajeev had also joined us. Gourav's house was filled with merriment and joy.

Shalini looked very pretty in her wedding dress. Gourav had invited most of his bookmaking fellows to the reception party, but that brought out the worst in the ceremony, which Gourav hadn't anticipated. Vivek also came with his parents. His presence enhanced the charm of the party; everyone wanted to click a picture with him. The relationship between Gourav and Vivek Mishra got highlighted to the bookmakers after his reception.

While Gourav was interacting with his guests, we sat on the lawn outside, talking. We were pulling Rajeev's leg, now that all of us had gone from being singular to being plural, except him? Rajeev chuckled, "Mummy and Papa are forcing me and telling me the same thing – all your friends got married, when will you? And now I am booked for the entire week to meet girls and their families," he said and stuffed his mouth with a dahi kabab.

"How many?" Curiously, I asked.

"Four. The moments my parents got to know that I was coming for a week, they fixed meetings," he said and picked up another kabab.

"Oho, so you will not have enough time for us, haan? *B*usy lad," I teased him.

We were all laughing.

"Aah... these dahi kababs are delicious. Nice arrangement, isn't it?" Rajeev said.

"All arrangements are done by the girl's side. Shalini is their only child and they wanted to make her wedding grand," Nitin said and asked the waiter to serve some cold drinks. Another waiter served chilli chicken on their table.

Nitin sipped his cold drink. "We really miss you in business. I just wish you could join us again," he told Rajeev.

"How is the business going?" Rajeev asked.

"Good. Actually, only Gourav handles most of the work. I cannot give enough time because of office. We are thinking of hiring one guy to operate the bhao line. He wants to build a good rapport in the industry. You can see that maximum of his guests are from this background. All of them are well settled in life, all are businessmen. Some of them are in real estate, some in textile, some are in gems business, and so on," Nitin said with excitement.

"But Gourav should also start something else, apart from this. I personally feel it cannot be one's career. Now that he is married, he will have more responsibilities. Do you think his career path is right? He has already lost a lot because of this in the past few months," Rajeev said.

"You are not wrong, Rajeev. I also feel that he should start a new business. Bookmaking should not be the end of his career, but give him some time.He has gone through a lot of losses in the last few months. Now give him some time to settle down first. I am happy he got a life partner, she will become his strength. And very soon he will take some good decisions. I am sure of that," Nitin said.

"Vivek helps Gourav, I know that, but it is unethical and illegal. In Mumbai, I heard a lot about match-fixing. There are very big names behind this fixing scandal. I am really scared sometimes. We started betting for our joy and we have reached so far, where gambling has been replaced by manipulating and fixing games." Rajeev paused and continued. "I read about the assassination of Sharad Shetty. Remember Sharad Shetty?" He looked in our eyes and helped us remember. "He was murdered just two months before the 2003 World Cup in South Africa. He was the greatest match-fixer and was working with Dawood Ibrahim. He had all the contact numbers and details of cricketers and gamblers. He was shot on the orders of Chhota Rajan, Dawood Ibrahim's rival. Chhota Rajan himself admitted in *Tehelka* magazine that the slaying of Sharad Shetty was his order. The objective was to gain revenge on Dawood as well as to get a foothold in the match-fixing market. These gangsters are still around the cricket world. There were so many players who received death threats from them," Rajeev lowered his voice and muttered.

Nitin kept his empty glass on the table and said, "We are very small bookmakers. The names you are taking are a different world in themselves. They don't need us and we don't need them. Vivek is like family, and he helps us because he knows Gourav's condition…" he was interrupted by Rajeev in between.

"And for this, he is taking remuneration," Rajeev said, but was interrupted by Nitin.

"Everyone is doing this, despite it being wrong. At least he is doing it for his brother. If we are earning good money with his help, then he should also get his share. Everyone wants more money, whether it's me, you, cricketers, film stars, politicians, everyone. We work hard in office and get a limited salary every month. Is that sufficient to enjoy our life? Don't we want more? Now, on whether it's right or wrong, for us this (bookmaking) is the only way to earn extra money. And yes, we have come far in this business. Suddenly if you stop this, it's not possible, my friend; it will take some time," Nitin said.

I noticed Nitin's face becoming heated while defending his stance. Though we were sitting under the open sky on a cold night, we were feeling warm after this heated discussion.

I interrupted Nitin. "It's okay, Nitin, but try to understand Rajeev's concern. What he is trying to say is to be honest in your business, because manipulating the game could be risky for you guys. Fixing is linked to the underworld. Big businessmen, celebrities, gangsters are associated with fixing scandals. Gourav and you do not come from a powerful background. What if you come into their sight? He is scared of that," I said.

"Yeah, we will be careful going ahead, and will escape safely if any adverse situation emerges… I promise. Thanks for your concern, Rajeev," Nitin said.

Rajeev brought a little smile on his face and said, "I just told you what was in my heart. We are true friends; it's our duty to guide each other. I didn't want to talk to Gourav about this because it is not the right time. It is a great moment in his life, and I do not want to ruin it. I trust you. Later on, you could speak to him about this, hmm?"

"Sure," Nitin promised and smiled.

"Now, let's go in. It's a time of merry-making and feasting. Let's see what special arrangements are done by the girl's side for the groom's friends." Rajeev egged us on for our bosom friend's wedding revelry.

Strange friend

Pushkar Mehta was talking over the phone to someone. 'Hmm'… 'How do you know that?'… 'When?'… 'He is a bookmaker?'… 'Okay'… 'It means he is close to him'… 'Where does he stay?'… 'Fine'… 'I want more information about him.'

He sat on his couch and dialled Satish Kaushik. "Gourav Mishra, do you know him?" he asked.

"Never heard of him before, who is he?" Satish replied.

"He is a bookie and also a relative of Vivek Mishra. Vivek came with his family to Gourav's wedding," Mehta said.

Satish commented, "A bookie is a relative of a cricketer. It sounds like a very co-operative relationship," and a wicked smile came on his face.

"My sources are gathering more information about them. It seems a bit difficult to directly approach Vivek Mishra, because ACSU and ICC always keep eye on their players, and because of them, they might feel uncomfortable dealing directly with us. This man Gourav could be the perfect go-between guy. I want you to connect with him."

"Okay, I'll try," Satish said.

Satish kept an eye on Gourav. Where he went, where his bookmaking centre was, who was in his family, where he liked to spend his time, and so on. Satish knew Naseef Ali, so he decided to meet Gourav through Naseef.

One day, Gourav was sitting with Naseef in a bar. Satish came and met Naseef, after which Naseef introduced Gourav to Satish. "Meet my friend, Gourav; he is also in our business. Gourav, meet Mr Satish! He is a big bookmaker, and he runs a real estate business as well."

Gourav shook hands with Satish and said, "It's a pleasure meeting you."

"So how long have you been in the bookmaking business?" Satish asked.

"Not very long, it's just been a year."

"And apart from this, what else do you do? Any other business you run?"

"Ahh, not right now."

Naseef told Gourav, "You can learn so much from Mr Satish. He is a very successful bookmaker."

Satish said gladly, "Look who is talking! He is already known as a big bookie, and he is praising me. Come on… We all are in the same industry, and I can just say that here, experience matters, and above all, luck… it's all luck."

Gourav agreed with him. "Truly said, it's all luck. But I am new here, I have far to go, and I need your suggestions and guidance. You people have good experience, I must learn from you."

"Any time… We can understand, we also started from somewhere, so don't worry, have faith in yourself. Take it easy," Satish said.

Naseef told Satish that Gourav is newly married.

Satish congratulated him. "Let me meet her some time. I would love to invite you both with family over for dinner. My wife and I will be happy if you guys come with your families," he said deliberately looking at Naseef and Gourav. They agreed.

The next day, Gourav reached Satish's house with Shalini. Naseef also came with his wife and three-year-old daughter. Satish introduced them to his wife Mona. After some time, Satish, along with Naseef and Gourav, came out into the lawn, leaving their wives to talk inside. His servant brought some drinks and snacks on his instruction. They were enjoying their drinks, and talking about each other.

Satish advised Gourav to start some business; a bookie should not only depend on bookmaking.

Gourav agreed and expressed his desire to open a medical store in the near future. He told them how he had left his job and started his business, and unfortunately had lost his shop and his land as well.

Heeding his hard-luck story, Satish offered to help Gourav in opening a medical store. He told him he could fund it. Gourav hesitated, saying he was sure he would be able to do it himself someday, and that he didn't need help.

But Satish insisted and said, "Don't hesitate. You can return the money whenever you feel comfortable. What is the use of money if it cannot help my friends? You can take it any time from me; it's yours only."

Gourav felt glad inside to get a great friend like him.

Satish poured some more whisky in the glasses and asked, "Where are you taking Shalini for your honeymoon?"

"Not decided yet..."

"Hmm. I would like to gift you a couple of tickets to Malaysia. Don't say no to this, it's my wedding gift to you," Satish said.

Gourav was stunned. "You haven't left me with any words Mr Satish… I am just speechless."

"And you don't have to say anything. I will send you the tickets, enjoy your honeymoon. Also after coming back, work on your dream project. Establish your shop; you don't have to worry about funds, I am telling you," Satish said with a right.

Gourav was overwhelmed. "Why are you doing all this? Today, I feel that I have got an elder brother in you," he said emotionally.

Satish interrupted him. "Don't worry, I will get a huge interest on all these, ha… ha… ha," he said and laughed. Gourav was also laughing.

When Shalini came to know that they were going to Malaysia for their honeymoon, she was very excited. She started planning their trip.

Nitin was happy to hear that Shalini and Gourav were going to Malaysia. In the evening, he came to meet them. Gourav told him all about Mr Satish.

He was all ears when Gourav was telling him the whole story. He thought for a while and asked, "Gourav, I am unable to understand. You met Satish just three days ago, and he gets so close to you that he is getting involved in your personal matters. Who is he? And why is he showing interest in you?"

"All I understood is that he is a good-hearted man and a great guy. He is a money man, a great bookmaker, and also in the real estate business. Helping others is not a big deal for him. I don't think I have anything in which he would be interested."

Nitin smiled and put his hand on his shoulder. "Yeah, you might be right. I was just asking because it sounded strange to me. But I am happy for you. Enjoy your honeymoon, have great fun. I will drop you guys to the airport." Nitin took his leave and went.

Nitin had doubts about Satish, but he didn't express them in front of Gourav; the time was not right for that. He called up Rajeev at night, and told him the whole story. Rajeev also agreed that without any motive, no one steps up to help. He must want something in return from Gourav.

"Gourav should not blindly believe Satish. Who knows his ulterior motive behind the help? You can't trust an acquaintance whom you met a few days before. You guys have been steeped in a world which is associated with illegal wagers and unsavoury characters. So be careful and alert. Have you ever met Satish?" Rajeev asked Nitin.

"Not yet, but I'm eager to meet him once. Gourav was revering him as a great money man."

After two days, Nitin went to Naseef and asked about Mr Satish in a very casual way. He asked him if he could meet him. Naseef told him that he had gone to Dubai for some days. He could meet him when he got back.

A high-profile party

Satish Kaushik was with Pushkar Mehta in Dubai to attend a party thrown by Shakeel Ahmad, an underworld don.

Shakeel Ahmad was leading an infamous crime syndicate, S-Company. He was accused of several bomb blasts, murders, cheating, match-fixing, etc, and was listed as India's most wanted criminal. He had been linked to Bollywood and the cricket world for ages. Celebrities wouldn't dare disobey him; on his one call, they came to attend his parties. He liked to throw grand parties, and famous faces added glamour to them.

A well-known Bollywood singer was singing popular songs on the stage and actors and actresses were dancing on the floor. Some industrialists were there too.

A fair man of average height, with a round moustachioed face was standing near the bar, a whisky glass in one hand and the other hand in his pocket, enjoying the song. At a glance, no one could gauge that this man was the most wanted criminal of India.

Shakeel Ahmad was accompanied by Shayam Kumar, a producer, and Reena Malik, an actress. Reena Malik had recently done a Shayam Kumar production, which was actually financed by Shakeel Ahmad. Hussain, one of his henchmen, happened to be passing by. Shakeel called him.

"Where is Bhatia?" Shakeel asked gruffly.

"Not here yet, I'll call him up now," Hussain said and dialled Punit Bhatia's number.

"Bhai, Bhatia is coming in a few minutes, he is nearby only."

"Hmm... Arrange the seating outside in the lawn. Send someone to take Bhatia there, I will be there soon," Shakeel said.

"All right," Hussain said and left.

Punit Bhatia was a big businessman and the owner of a cricket team by the name "East Royal Champions" in BPL (Bharat Premier League). The BPL was going to be held in a few months, and the auction of cricket players was going to start from the next month. Shakeel had something in mind and that's why he wanted to meet Punit Bhatia.

His minion received Punit Bhatia and took him to the lawn. He sat on the chair, and a waiter came and placed two whisky glasses and some appetisers on the table. Shakeel soon arrived. He shook hands with Bhatia and offered him whisky. "Cheers." Both clinked their glasses together.

"Nice party," Bhatia said.

A smile appeared on Shakeel's face. He signalled the waiter to put some more ice in the drink and leave.

"So, all set for BPL?" Shakeel tasted his drink and asked.

"Yeah, we will have some meetings next week for the coming auction. There we will discuss the strategy."

"Hmm." After a pause, Shakeel uttered, "I am thinking of investing in your team this time."

Shakeel's words dropped a bombshell on Bhatia. He was stunned for a moment. His hand holding the whisky glass remained still near his mouth. He looked at Shakeel, who was looking at his own glass seriously. Things were running fast in his mind. Shakeel's involvement meant a lot of things. It might give the impression that he wears the trousers but it's Shakeel who will make the final decisions. But in spite of that, he did not have the courage to deny him. So he wore a fake smile and said, "Bhai, this team is all yours. Tell me what kind of investment you want."

"Last year, your team reached the semi-finals. This time, I want you to win the final. Hussain will give you a list of players who must be in your team; I will provide you their price whatever it is. You won't have to hesitate in making higher bids, got it?" Shakeel said in his gruff voice.

Bhatia clinched the deal in no time. "All right, I believe you. If you have chosen, then they will be the finest ones."

Shakeel called Hussain to hand over the list of players to Bhatia.

Bhatia looked at the list. There were three foreign players listed, of which one was a batsman and two were fast bowlers. The rest were Indian players; two batsmen and one spinner.

"Perfect, bhai. Good selection, must say." Bhatia grinned.

"So you are agreeing with the list?" Shakeel asked for confirmation.

"Of course, they are the best. How about including Vivek Mishra in the batting line, along with Kiran Walia, and Watson Geek?" he asked enthusiastically.

"Watson and Kiran could be good choices, but I won't suggest Vivek. His performance is low these days. Surya Chand of Sri Lanka could be a much better choice instead of him," Shakeel said.

"Right bhai." Bhatia nodded.

"Let's go inside, the party is on… come," Shakeel said and they went inside the party hall.

Inside the hall, fast music was playing. Pushkar was standing in a corner. He went to Shakeel and touched his feet to show respect.

"Pushkar! How are you, man? And all good?" Shakeel asked gruffly.

"All well, bhai… it's all your blessings."

"How is the party?" He usually asked to hear his own praise and people left no stone unturned to flatter him.

"It's splendid, like always," Pushkar looked around and said.

After a pause, he said, "Bhai, there is a problem, and I need your help in this."

"Hmm, speak."

"My ten crores have been blocked in hawala by Guru Rajan," he said.

Guru Rajan was the leader of Guru Gang, and Shakeel's rival in the underworld.

"The funds were coming from Karachi to Mumbai, and it was being delayed. After some time, I got to know that some associates of Guru Gang had been blocking that. Bhai, it's only you who can unblock my money," Pushker pleaded.

Shakeel listened to him and said, "I'll ask Hussain to look over your matter. It will get solved soon, don't worry. Guru Rajan is a bastard! Only these little things could be expected of him."

Shakeel went on to meet other guests. The party was on till midnight; guests were taking their leave of Shakeel and thanking him for the party. When Bhatia came to him, he whispered in his ear, "Remember what we discussed. We have to make a huge profit this time." Bhatia smiled and shook hands with him.

Two different ways

Gourav and Shalini brought a gift for Satish from Malaysia to express their gratitude to him. Gourav asked Shalini to invite him and Mona for dinner. Shalini had prepared some special dishes for the evening, and they presented the gifts they had brought for them.

In a few days, both the families got very close to each other. Gourav liked to spend his time with Satish and also took tips from him in his bookmaking business. Satish egged him on to start his own business. Gourav was again thinking to open a pharmacy, which was his dream.

However, Nitin cautioned him many times that too much closeness with Satish was not good, and taking funds for his business would make him obliged to Satish forever.

One day, Nitin was trying to convince Gourav of the same thing, but Gourav was being stubborn. He told him, "What is wrong if he wants to help me? Satish has now become my good friend, like you, Rajeev, and Amit. You guys have helped me a lot in the past, I always felt free to share my happiness and problems with you guys. Just like that, I shared my problems with Satish and he himself offered to help. If I refuse, he might feel bad."

"I discussed it with Rajeev and Amit. We all want that you set up your business and settle down. You need money for that... We will help you in this, you have to just wait for some time, and everything will be on track. You need not go to someone else," Nitin said in a soft tone.

"Buddy! I have to prove myself before Shalini's family. You can't understand how much it hurts. I don't want to wait for long now, especially when opportunity is knocking on my door. And you guys have already helped me when I was in need; I also want to pay you back as soon as possible. Satish is not 'someone else' for me. I know him very well. I can start my shop again with his help in no time, then what should I wait for? You will see, very soon I will be capable of returning his money," Gourav said.

"How can I make you understand? Your madness has made you blind, you do not trust us, but that fickle man who is showing you his money," Nitin said in irritation.

"You are barking up the wrong tree. You don't like Satish. I got that, but it doesn't mean he is a bad guy. I don't know why you are jealous of him." Gourav raised his voice this time.

"Why should I be jealous of him, I don't even know him! I am just concerned for you. I saw you becoming hopeless and struggling in your bad days. You don't put a foot wrong, don't get into any trouble, I only want that." His voice got emotional with his last sentence.

"Okay, tell me what trouble is waiting for me? What is it you knew that I don't, I want to ask you today," he said in an irritating way.

"I wish I could explain all these things to you, but not today, you won't get my point," Nitin said.

"Why? Why can't I understand? Because you don't have enough reasons to justify your point!" He became restive.

"No. Because you are in your dream world, and you are not ready to listen to any external voice," Nitin said tautly.

Their conversation had become fierce. Both were getting edgy in their words and manner.

Gourav's patience was wearing thin. He said annoyingly, "Yes, I have my dreams, and you have problems with it… I can sniff it out. You don't care for me, but you have problems with my progress. Otherwise, there would be happiness on your face rather than this strain."

Nitin yelled, "Enough! Please stop this nonsense. It's entire my fault that I tried to tell you what I felt was wrong. Sorry." He went out of the room and slammed the door behind him in a rage.

Nitin left the place, very disturbed. Gourav's words had been hurting him all day.

Nitin had got an offer from a banking company some days back, the posting was in Mumbai. Neha and Rajeev advised him to take this offer. But Nitin thought he should also discuss it with Gourav once before accepting it. That day, he had gone to Gourav to tell him about this new opportunity, but instead of that, they had ended up fighting.

Nitin took the decision. He decided to accept the offer and move to Mumbai.

Nitin didn't talk to Gourav for a week. He kept himself busy in fulfilling the formalities of joining the new job.

Some days later, Gourav came to Nitin's house. Nitin was not there, so Neha talked to him for long. She told him that they were moving to Mumbai. Gourav was shocked to hear this. It was also strange for Neha that Gourav had no idea about their shifting, that Nitin had not told him anything about. After some time, Nitin arrived. Neha left them to talk and went in the kitchen to bring some tea and snacks.

"You didn't tell me that you are changing your job and shifting to Mumbai," Gourav said, looking into his eyes.

Nitin looked out of the window. After a few seconds, he said, "I wanted to tell you about it, but didn't get the chance…"

Gourav was still looking into his eyes. "And you kept things within!" After a pause, he said, "Actually I was stupid! I was only interested in talking about myself. I didn't ask anything about you. Sorry for that day. I misbehaved with you, sorry!"

"Come on… We are friends and it happens in friendship… So don't be sorry. I also crossed my limit, which I should not have." Nitin hugged him. Their eyes became moist. Neither of them had had an easy time since they skirmished.

"Then why are you going to Mumbai? I will be left alone here," Gourav said emotionally.

"I have to go now; don't have an option. At the end of the month, we will leave."

"And what about our partnership?" Gourav asked.

"From now onwards, that's all yours."

"What nonsense! How can I handle everything? You know that I need you… First Rajeev and now you, everyone is leaving me one by one," Gourav said.

Nitin stood up and went to the window to close it, it was becoming dark outside, and then he said, "Other people are around you, so you won't feel alone. Satish, Naseef, they are also with you. It's a cycle of life, friends come and go. New friends take the place of old friends."

"I know you are upset, but old friends are jewels," Gourav said.

"If I really mean so much to you, then I want to give you some advice," Nitin said. "It was I who involved you in this betting game, but then I didn't have any idea that we would come so far in this and run it like a business. Now I feel, we should stop all this. I don't know why I am getting a bad intuition these days. It's time to get rid of all this gambling and betting; we are not made for such things. People from the underworld, criminals, powerful and big names are involved in cricket fixing, so leave this."

Gourav took a deep breath and said, "You know, Nitin, bookmaking is not my passion or hobby, it's my bread and butter. I don't have an alternative option for earning like you, that's why I want to start my shop as soon as possible. I also don't want to be dependent on bookmaking only. Until I set up my business, I can't leave this."

After some days, Nitin shifted to Mumbai with Neha and joined his new company. After Nitin left, Gourav hired two more persons to handle the work pressure. With Satish's help, he opened a new chemist shop called 'Gourav Medicals'.

PART III

I reached home by 11 p.m. I found a kind of resentment in the air most of the guests had left after waiting for me, mummy was upset, trying to read a Hindi magazine, papa was taking a catnap on the sofa, some of my cousins were watching a movie on the TV.

"Amit bhaiya has come, Amit bhaiya has come!" they shouted in excitement, and came to hug me.

Papa woke up from his slumber, adjusted his specs and slippers, came to me and asked, "How is Gourav now?"

"Still in the same condition, doctors are doing their job."

"And do the police have any information about the attackers? Who were they?" he asked.

"Not yet," I said slowly.

"You seem very tired. Take some rest now," he said on seeing me gloomy. He turned to my cousins who wanted to chat with me. "Children, Amit is tired from the travel, and it's already very late, so let him take some rest. You also go and sleep. Tomorrow you can talk to him as much as you wish."

Mom was irritated. "All the relatives and neighbours left, after waiting for long. Couldn't you have gone to the hospital tomorrow? Everyone was asking for you, and we had to explain to everyone."

"Oh ho! They will come later, let it be. Now arrange dinner for everyone," Papa told mom.

"I prepared everything for you and Richa. Is this the time to have dinner? No one will eat properly," she cribbed and went into the kitchen.

"Where is Richa"? I asked Papa.

"We sent her to take some rest in her room. She had been meeting the guests ever since she stepped in. You also go, get fresh and come to the dining table, call Richa also."

Mom was a little upset, so to lighten her mood, I asked Richa to present the gifts we had brought for her and all the others. I thought that was the best way to coax her. At the dining table, we handed over their gifts to them. Mom's face lit up to see her gifts; a beautiful green Jadeite beads necklace for her, which she liked very much. After distribution of gifts, we had our dinner, and talked till late in the night.

Next morning, I woke up around 11.30 a.m. due to jet lag. Richa somehow managed to wake up a bit early and now she was helping mom in the kitchen. After freshening up, mom served me breakfast. "Where is the newspaper?" I asked mom. She gave the newspaper to me

I turned the pages, the paper was filled with the story of cricket match-fixing scandals; the raids and arrest of bookies, suspected names of players and renowned persons, involvement of businessmen and gangsters, clues and chain of the network, etc, etc.

There was some news on the third page which caught my eyes, it was about Gourav.

A Delhi businessman and bookie, Gourav Mishra, is still critical, after being stabbed by some unknown attackers three

days back, when he went to pick up his bike from the parking lot after shutting down his shop around 11 pm.

He was running a bookmaking centre also, but in the recent past, he had provided some vital information and links to the police about this illegal business which has corrupted India's most worshipped sport, cricket. With his help, the police had lifted the lid off many undercover facts and had been able to capture a number of illegal bookmaking centres. After a probe, the police are stating that some notable elements could be behind this attack. Police is not denying the involvement of underworld in this. But still, in the absence of concrete evidence, no names have been declared yet.'

"Amit, there is a phone call for you." Mom's voice rang in my ears.

I picked up the phone; it was Nitin on the other side.

"Rajeev reached today morning and eagerly wants to meet you. He's coming to my house and together we will go to the hospital. When are you coming?"

"I will also reach there by lunch-time."

Mom was sitting nearby, chopping vegetables. She interrupted immediately. "No, no, you are not going nowhere. Your Dhiraj mama and mami are coming, and so is Rakhi bua. Yesterday, already so many guests left without meeting you." Her tone was stern.

"Mom, Rajeev has come from Mumbai," I said.

"You can go later in the evening, once they leave. It doesn't look good if they come to see you and you aren't at home," mom said.

I agreed with her in spite of wanting to spend time with my friends.

When I reached the hospital, it was 6:30 p.m. I saw the police talking to Gourav's family members; Nitin and Rajeev were also around them. I walked quickly to overhear their conversation.

The police were carrying some papers and wanted to know whether those were written by Gourav or not. They had found those letters in a farm house in Faridabad. Those letters were addressed to Shalini, to his father, to his mother, to Nitin, and also to Rajeev.

We confirmed that it was Gourav's handwriting. But the question which was running in almost everyone's mind was why and when he had written all those letters?

The police wanted to keep them as evidence for further investigation, but on the request of all, they allowed us some time to read those letters and afterwards the police would take them in their custody.

We exchanged those letters turn by turn and went through them. And the other side of my fun loving, jaunty buddy was revealed to me. I came to know that he was very sensitive! Shalini and Gourav's mother even cried after reading them. He had opened his heart in those letters. And only a true heart could do that. He had confessed his mistakes, confessed his fears and confessed his perplexity; depicted his love towards Shalini, his parents and friends.

Lastly, the letters revealed many untold facts of his life.

Falling into the wrong hands

After separating from Nitin, Gourav had opened his shop once again. Satish had helped him to get a foot in the door and had established a special place in Gourav's life. Gourav had also ensconced Satish as his mentor in his heart.

After three months, BPL started. Vivek Mishra was in the 'Central Tigers' team. He was passing information related to his own team and others to Gourav from time to time. Satish was also taking advantage of his friendship with Gourav, as Gourav was sharing information with him also.

One day, Satish insisted Gourav to come along with him to meet Pushkar Mehta, the head of the betting syndicate in India. He was in Delhi for a few days only; after that he was going to Dubai.

"Where are we going to meet him?" Gourav asked.

"To his farm house in Faridabad; it will take hardly forty minutes to reach," Satish said, while driving the car.

"I am feeling a little awkward. What will I do there? We don't even know each other."

"Don't worry. I've already tell him that I have a friend with me. And you should know the industry, my dear! You should feel privileged that you are meeting high-profile persons!" Satish said emphasising each and every word.

They reached the farm house.

Pushkar was sitting in the hall and watching the BPL match between 'Southern Coast Riders' and 'Gladiator West' on the screen. Satish and Gourav entered the hall.

"Come, come, I was waiting for you. Welcome Gourav, meeting you for the first time, but I've heard about you from Satish so many times!" Pushkar said with a smile.

Gourav shook hands with Pushkar and said, "I have also heard lots about you from Satish. It's really nice meeting you, sir!"

After some formal talk, Pushkar asked Gourav, "I heard Vivek Mishra is your cousin, is it?"

A wry smile appeared on Gourav's face because he never wanted to disclose his intimacy with Vivek to everyone. "Yes sir, we are brothers," he said grudgingly.

"Then it is very easy for you to fetch updates of matches," Pushkar said.

Gourav hesitated for a while and looked at Satish. Satish smiled with ease.

Gourav took a deep breath and said, "Nothing is hidden from you, sir, but it's not like that. Yes, sometimes his information works for me, but I can't take advantage of him every time.We both know our limits," he spoke in a defensive way.

Pushkar laughed. "Limits! Really? Okay, tell me, what is your limit? Using information in betting… or spot fixing… or match-fixing?" He said, rotating the TV remote with his left hand's fingers.

Gourav was stunned for a while, for it was the most unexpected question. "What are you saying, sir?" He somehow managed to utter.

"Why are you making a fool of yourself?" He kept the remote back on his side, put his right leg upon his left leg and said, "I had already doubted that Vivek plays for someone. Most of the time, his game does not seem genuine. And I came to know that it is you."

"Sir... I think there is some confusion," Gourav defended himself.

"I don't, my dear. I don't like to talk about baseless things. I know everything about you. I have done my research on you. It's you who called him up regularly from different numbers during tournaments, and used code words like bull, bunny, super fast train, etc. You easily make money from updated information during odds, and sometimes, you manipulate his game also, am I right?" he said, looking straight into his eyes.

Gourav didn't look away. He gathered his courage and asked directly, "What do you want from me?"

"Work for us. You will earn much more."

Suddenly, Pushkar's phone rang; he excused himself and went outside to take his call.

Inside the room, Gourav burst out at Satish. "Satish, what the hell is all this?"

Satish said calmly, "Calm down, Gourav. Don't react like this. Pushkar Mehta is a big name, and like a godfather to me. I also used to do whatever he told me to, so I'll advise you to do the same."

"But why should I? I don't want to get into all this," Gourav expressed his dissent.

"Money matters a lot, Gourav, do it for money. Don't you want to enjoy life with Shalini? Money can fetch every joy and happiness for you. In this world, if you have money, you are the king. And lots of money in this game. Trust me and say yes," Satish tried to tantalise him.

Gourav thought for a while and said, "But this time it will be risky to talk to Vivek, and I can't assure you that I would be able to convince him for deals."

"The deal which Pushkar throws is difficult to reject; you don't bother about that. He needs you because there is risk to talk directly with any player now, but it is not difficult for you. The first thing is that you are his cousin. If two brothers are talking, then no one suspects, and secondly, you know very well how to communicate with him, you are the right person for this work," Satish said.

Pushkar Mehta returned.

"So are you ready to work with us?" Pushkar asked and sat on his chair.

"What is the deal?" Gourav asked.

Pushkar grinned. "Day after tomorrow, the match is between 'Central Tigers' and 'Gladiator West'. The fast bowler Rozer De Souza will throw three consecutive no balls when Vivek will be on his strike. He could do that in his second or third over. And Vivek will have to hit those balls for sixes," he said.

Gourav was shocked. "Rozer De Souza will be doing this?"

"Yes. Before throwing the no ball, he will give a sign. Usually, he tucks a handkerchief on the right side of his trouser. At that point of time, he will take off his handkerchief, rub the ball with it and keep it in his back pocket. And that will be the sign of three no balls. For this, Vivek Mishra will be paid fifty lakh rupees, and you will get 30% of the amount. Is that okay?" He said.

Gourav thought, it's not a bad deal, and it won't affect Vivek's performance anymore. So he nodded and agreed to the deal.

Pushkar continued, "You have to convey this message to Vivek. How? You know best. One more thing, I can't bear any confusion in this, so be very clear. One mistake and deal cancelled."

"I know…you don't worry."

Satish and Gourav left soon after.

Outside, Gourav asked Satish, "You knew all these things, right? You brought me here deliberately for this spot-fixing and all? And I was thinking you were my well-wisher."

"I am still your well-wisher. Aren't you benefitting from this, tell me?" Satish asked.

Gourav ignored him, "I will have to talk to Vivek. I hope I get a chance."

Satish said emphatically. "Yes, get the chance, anyhow. If necessary, meet him personally, but you have to do it. Now you are working for Pushkar Mehta. He is a person who does things by hook or by crook. He has considerable muscle power associated with him; it's not easy to deny him. So convince Vivek anyhow.

"And remember, money is a thing. Whoever has it is also busy making more and more; there is no end to desire. I need money, you need money, and similarly, he will also want more money. Be confident in yourself, buddy. You are offering him loads of money and he has to do a mere favour in return, that's it," Satish said. "You are the new kid on the block, but don't worry, I will polish you up," he patted his shoulder with a smile.

It was the ninth time since afternoon when Gourav dialled Vivek's number. Every time, it was switched off; but luckily, this time the call got connected. Gourav wanted to meet him the next day, but Vivek was in Kolkata, busy with a tight schedule of practice session and it was not possible for him to meet Gourav. But Gourav insisted that he meet him anyhow, they could not talk over the phone. At last, Vivek agreed to meet him at 8 o'clock for dinner.

Next morning, Gourav took a flight and reached Kolkata. In the evening, he was waiting for Vivek in the hotel. At nearly 8 o'clock, Vivek reached there.

Vivek directly shot his question as he sat on the chair, "What is so important, why did you call me? Don't you know it could create trouble for me?"

"Yeah, I know, but it couldn't be discussed over the phone. I have an offer of fifty lakh rupees for you." Gourav kept his voice low.

"Fifty lakhs… for what?" Vivek asked.

"Tomorrow, you have to hit three consecutive sixes to Rozer De Souza's bowling," Gourav lowered his voice as much as possible.

Vivek's brow was furrowed in confusion "Come again… be clear," he asked.

"De Souza will bowl three consecutive no balls and you will hit them for sixes. You will get the sign from him, probably in his second or third over. He will take out his towel from his right side, rub the ball and keep it in his back pocket," Gourav whispered.

Vivek was stupefied to hear it. "Is it? So do you have a deal with De Souza also?" he asked in amazement.

"You can think so," Gourav said hesitantly.

"I can't believe it. Really? Gourav… Buddy, you are becoming a fixer gradually. Hmm… Fifty lakhs. Not bad… and how much are you paying to De Souza? And how… how did you do that?" Vivek was amazed with Gourav's proposal, and had so many questions.

Gourav didn't want Vivek to know that he was a go-between guy, and was working for a top syndicate, so he was avoiding answering his queries. At the same time, some of Vivek's team members entered. Seeing Vivek there, they came to him and exclaimed, "Buddy! You already here… and nobody knows you are enjoying food alone."

Vivek laughed and introduced Gourav to them, "Meet my cousin, Gourav. He is in the city just for today. So we planned to have dinner out."

One of them said, "We heard that the food is delicious here, so we came. It's nice that you guys are also here." With that, they dragged some chairs around and sat together at the same table. Gourav felt relaxed in the sudden emerged company of his favourite cricketers where he got a clean escape from Vivek's curious questions. They ordered food and dined together.

Gourav had a flight, so he rushed to the airport soon after.

The next morning was crucial for him; he was on tenterhooks. If everything went according to plan, then he could make a tremendous amount of money. On the other hand, rain on the parade would make his life hell. He could bear the loss somehow, but he also had a tiger by the tail. What would he do if the tiger got annoyed?

Gourav reached his centre; his boys were sitting in the office and keeping their eyes on odds and bets. Gourav's cell phone rang; it was Satish.

Satish asked instantly, “All set?”

“Yes,” replied Gourav.

“Good! Risk?”

“I have put in all my effort. Next is luck,” Gourav replied.

“Hmm, ok,” and he cut the call.

The match between Central Tigers v/s Gladiator West had started. Gladiator West was batting first. The team made 124 runs on the loss of 6 wickets.

In the second innings, Central Tigers lost its first wicket at 30 runs in the sixth over. Vivek Mishra came to take the strike, and played a defensive game rather than aggressive; he made only six runs out of eleven balls. The commentators were disparaging because the run rate was running low. In the tenth over, Rozer De Souza took charge of bowling. Vivek faced two balls in that over.

Rozer again took charge in the 12th over, when Vivek was on strike. Rozer measured his balling point from the wicket, marked a line from his shoes… Suddenly, Vivek saw that he had taken his towel from his right side and started rubbing the ball. He thought, ‘is that the sign of no ball’? Rozer tucked the towel into his trouser’s back pocket and started running. Oh! He did it in the same manner that Gourav had told him yesterday. Vivek was relating things rapidly in his mind. I have to hit these balls for sixes, mid off would be a better option, and with this, he hit the ball out of the boundary. The stadium applauded, the umpire signalled a no ball. The next ball was also a no ball; Vivek hit that for a six again. Two consecutive sixes made the audience go crazy. Now everyone was curious about a hat-trick.

The betting market was up and running. Odds were set high; huge bets were placed on the next ball of De Souza. Would the next ball be no ball again? Would it be a six again? The betting segment crossed its fingers.

De Souza threw the third no ball, and Vivek hit the ball for a six again. "A beautiful shot on log off entered the crowd, fabulous," the commentator said. "It's an unbelievable third no ball from Rozer De Souza and Vivek didn't miss the chance. He took full advantage and made the hat-trick."

Gourav heaved a sigh of relief; he won bets thick and fast. That day proved to be good for him. Next day, all the transactions were placed through hawala. Satish came to his workplace and handed over the cash.

"Pushkar is extremely happy with you. He is on cloud nine; you made the day," Satish said.

"Yes, we all have earned enough. But Satish, I want to let you know that I will not bear that much risk now. I respect you and Mr Mehta a lot and all I did was just because of that. But further on, I wouldn't prefer to accept these types of spot-fixing deals. I want to be clear on this," Gourav said.

"You should be feeling honoured to work with Mr Mehta. Today you have plenty of money in your hand. Just think about what you were before. Every time, the bookmaking business just tantalised you. And what happened the last time? You were left starved for every penny. Today, many bookies and punters would be in the red after losing yesterday's bet, but see, you are not among them. Don't bother about risk and all. Gradually, you will know that Pushkar Mehta is a personality. He doesn't twist anyone's arm in vain. Rather than being pernickety, be a complacent person," Satish said and handed over another packet to Gourav, which had Vivek's share.

Fixing in Chennai

Punit Bhatia's team 'East Royal Champions' was performing well and had the highest point to enter the semi-finals. Other teams which perhaps could qualify for semi-finals were 'Central Tigers', 'Southern Coast Riders', 'Himalayan Heights' or 'King's Paradise'. 'Central Tigers' was also at its peak and was the strongest contester to qualify for semi-finals. Its next match was with 'Himalayan Heights' and whoever won, could enter directly into the semi-finals and would play against 'East Royal Champions'.

'Central Tigers' batted first and scored 130 runs for the loss of 3 wickets. Vivek Mishra remained not out and scored 56 runs. 'Himalayan Heights' tried to chase the score bravely, but 'Central Tigers' didn't let them succeed and won the match by nine runs. With this, 'Central Tigers' entered the semi-finals.

That evening, Punit Bhatia received a call from Shakeel Ahmad.

Shakeel said, "Your team has to reach the finals. 'Central Tigers' has shown a wonderful performance in the tournament matches. Do you think your team could beat them in the semi-finals?"

Bhatia said, "Bhai, though I have a very strong team, I am not too confident about the result. It's unpredictable."

"That match is very important for me, so don't take any chances. Tell your players that everyone has to play to win. If they win the BPL trophy, I will gift a bungalow in Dubai, to each and every player," Shakeel said.

Bhatia seconded him, "Perfect bhai. I'll place this offer before them. My instinct says we will win."

Bhatia called a meeting with the players, and bragged, "My best wishes to you all for your upcoming match. I am proud of my team; you have played well and reached the semi-finals. Only two matches are left to win the BPL trophy, and I am very sure that 'East' will grab the trophy this year. Does everyone have the same fire?"

"Yeah, sure we will..." the players said in chorus.

Bhatia steered them. "You guys need to play a strong game while facing 'Central Tigers'. They have turned into a ball of fire, and they will put all their efforts against us. So this match is very crucial for our team. I will gift everyone a bungalow in Dubai, if you win the finals. I give you my word."

Next day brought bad news for 'East Royal Champions'. By some twist of fate, one of its opening batsmen got injured during practice. Watson Geek, the opening batsman in tremendous form, fractured his right elbow. Doctors advised him to take rest for at least thirty days. Therefore, he would not be able to play in the semi-finals or finals. Watson Geek's dismissal could be a great scourge for the team. Punit Bhatia knew that, and he called up Hussain to let him know about it.

Hussain went to Shakeel and told him about the injury and dismissal of Watson Geek.

Shakeel asked him to send a message to Reena Malik that he wanted to talk to her. After that, he made a call to Pushkar Mehta.

Shakeel asked Pushkar, "Did you get the news that Watson Geek won't be playing in the semi-finals?"

"Bhai, I know that," Pushkar said.

"How would the market be?"

"Market would be very lucrative after this information. I think… bets will be placed thick and fast in favour of 'Central Tigers'," Pushkar replied.

"I am gambling on 'East Royal Champions' and its winning is important for me. Three days are left for the match. Can you provide me the details about where the 'Central Tigers' team will be staying in Chennai?" Shakeel asked.

"Yes, I have the information. Tonight, the team will reach the Taj hotel. Tomorrow, they have a four-hour practice session," Pushkar replied.

Curious, he asked again, "If you don't mind, bhai, may I know whether fixing is involved in this? Is the match in the favour of 'East Royal Champions'?"

"Yeah, it is. I want to buy some 'Central Tiger' players too. You have a good contact. I am sending Reena Malik to Chennai for this work, help her out," Shakeel said.

Then Shakeel talked to Reena.

"I want you to be in Chennai during the semi-finals. Postpone all your assignments for two to three days."

"No problem, bhai… tell me, what can I do for you?" Reena accepted his command without any ifs or buts.

"'Central Tigers' team will be staying at the Taj hotel. You have to persuade three players for spot-fixing – Vivek Mishra, Fazal Mahmood, and Donald Steve. Pushkar will help you in this. Be careful because ACSU always has eyes on these players. Hussain will let you know the rest of the details about the deal and all," Shakeel told her.

Reena packed her stuff quickly and rushed to the airport. One of Hussain's people handed her the ticket. After two-and-a-half hours, she reached Chennai. Satish Kaushik was waiting for her.

"How was your flight?" Satish asked.

"It was fine. How else could it be, on such a short notice?" Reena said and laughed.

"Yeah, and in a very short time, lots of things have to materialise," Satish said.

"Hmm… So what is the strategy?"

"You have to deal with three players only – Vivek Mishra, Fazal Mahmood and Donald Steve. Shekhar Dhanraj will help introduce you to them; he is a photographer with the Indian cricket team. Just remember, he will only introduce you to them; he has nothing to do with the deals, and you don't have to tell him anything from your side," Satish said.

Reena nodded and asked, "Well… what is the deal?"

"Yeah, I am coming to that. Fazal Mahmood, the captain, and Vivek Mishra, both are batsmen. They shouldn't make more than twenty-five runs in the match. Donald Steve is a bowler. He has to give fourteen runs in a certain over. They will get eighty-five lakhs for it," Satish said and handed her a cell phone. "Keep this; you can talk to me and Hussain bhai using this number. I fed both our numbers in the phone. During the deal, we will use only these numbers to communicate. Hope everything is clear to you?"

Reena nodded.

After collecting room keys for Reena and confirming that Shekhar had also checked-in, Satish turned to Reena and said, "You go and freshen up, till then I will meet Shekhar. I will take him down to the common area. You also come there by 4:30 p.m."

Satish went to meet Shekhar.

Shekhar let him in and asked, "How are you? I was boarding the flight when you called, so I couldn't talk much. All good?"

Satish replied, "Yeah, actually something important came up, that's why I am troubling you. I want some help from you."

Shekhar offered him water and asked, "What is it?"

"Do you know the actress Reena Malik?"

Shekhar tried to remember the name. "Re…ee…na ma…lik. Yes, I've heard this name; she might have done a movie recently, around one month ago."

"Yes, that's her. You have to help introduce her to cricketers," Satish said as a command.

"Why should I? I don't even know her," Shekhar thought for a second and said.

"Ahh, she is in the same hotel, and you will meet her very soon. You know cricketers and it's easy for you to make the introduction," Satish said coolly.

Shekhar wasn't able to understand. "Why does she want to meet… and why will I make the introduction? You do know it is not my job."

Satish pulled out a bundle of notes from his handbag and kept it in Shekhar's hand. "You don't need to get into all this. You just do what I am telling you. Keep this with you; it's for your job... You can get more after the work."

Shekhar wondered, looking at the money. "What are you doing? What is this?"

"To introduce someone to others is not a crime. And I am offering you money because in today's world, nobody will do anything for anyone free of cost. Keep this and stop thinking too much. She is a celebrity and you are a photographer. It's not odd. If you make one celebrity meet other celebrities, what is wrong in this?" Satish tried to convince him.

The thick bundle of notes had shaken Shekhar's integrity. "Okay, where is she?" he asked.

"Come with me," and they both came down to the common area.

Reena joined them in some time. Shekhar told them that the players would come to the restaurant for dinner when they reach by 8 p.m.

By 8:15 p.m, the team reached the hotel. Their coach instructed them to take their keys, freshen up and come down for dinner.

In the restaurant, Reena Malik was waiting for the players. She was dressed in a yellow evening gown and looked charming. Shekhar joined her and told her that the players would be coming in a few minutes. Gradually, the players started coming. Reena knew most of the Indian players, but not some of the foreign players.

Reena asked him. "Who is Fazal Mahamood among them?"

"The man with the cap is Fazal Mahamood," Shekhar said.

Fazal had seen Shekhar talking to some lady. He looked at her and wasn't able to take his eyes off her face. He asked Amit Yogi if he knows the stunner sitting with Shekhar.

With that, Amit and Surya looked in the direction where Reena and Shekhar were seated.

"Yeah, she is gorgeous. Who is she?" Amit said.

"I saw they were talking about us… let's go, we should meet them," Fazal said.

Surya wanted a drink, so he moved to the bar.

Fazal and Amit reached their table. "Hey Shekhar, how are you doing, man?"

Shekhar stood up and shook hands with them. "I am doing well," he said with a smile.

Fazal continued, "I liked the picture you clicked in Kolkata, the match with 'Gladiator West'… that was superb. I want a copy for myself in 7'5"size. Could you please do it for me?"

Shekhar was glad. "Yes, sure I will," he pledged.

Fazal smiled, and looking at Reena, he asked Shekhar, "Won't you introduce us to the pretty lady?"

"She is Reena Malik, an actress. Her film released last month. Sheis doing some Tamil films also."

Reena said hello and shook hands with Fazal and Amit. "It's a pleasure meeting you," she said with a smile.

"Same here. If you don't mind, can we sit here?"

"Yeah, sure," she said, happy at the turn of events.

"So, are you new to the industry?" Fazal asked, looking into her eyes.

"I am here since the last three years."

"Oh! Actually, we don't get too much time from our busy schedule. I think that's why I missed your films. By the way, which was the recent one?" Fazal asked.

"The Queen of Hearts."

"Is it? Nice title, it must be a nice movie. After BPL, I will take a break and watch your movies."

Amit saw that Fazal was showing a lot of interest in Reena, so he thought he'd leave the place. Shekhar went with him. Now, Reena and Fazal were left at the table. Reena had a great chance to go ahead with her plan.

"You are looking gorgeous," Fazal admired her.

Reena ruffled her hair gently with a smile and said, "Thanks."

She asked, "So you must have tough competition from 'East' in the coming match."

Fazal wondered and asked with a smile, "Are you following BPL?"

"Yeah, I watch it sometimes."

"East is in full form, and yeah, I hope it will be a good match. We are also doing well, aren't we? By the way, which is your favourite team?" Fazal asked her.

Reena diverted his attention. "Shall we pick some food for ourselves?" she said.

"Yup, let's go."

Fazal asked again, "You didn't tell me yet. Which team is your favourite?"

"I don't have any particular choice. I am not a cricket buff. I know very little about it."

"That's rude," Fazal said in an offended way, then smiled and said, "Just kidding. I also don't like to talk about the game all the time. So, tell me about yourself. What are you doing in Chennai?"

Reena took a break from eating and said, "I am here for some important work; as soon as it finishes, I will return. I was getting bored here and thanks to you for a nice company today."

"No thanks…"

"No, I really mean it, I'm having a good time with you," Reena emphasised her words.

Fazal smiled and asked, "Are you free tomorrow at lunch time?"

"Yes, I am in the hotel only," she said.

"If you don't mind, can we have lunch together?" Fazal asked and looked at her, desperate for her nod.

Reena smiled and nodded, "Okay."

"We have a practice session in the morning, after that I will give you a call. What is your room number?" Fazal added.

"311, 3rd floor," Reena told him. They finished their dinner, and Reena bade goodbye for the night.

Next day, after the team practice, Fazal booked a table for lunch at a hotel. Reena was ready on time to go out with him. She wore a knee length skirt and a strap-less bare-shoulder orange top.

They went together in a car. The whole way, Fazal was admiring her and flirting with her. Reena just gave him a smile and spoke little. Her smile gave him the wrong signal. He pulled her hand towards him and kissed it gently. Reena didn't protest and allowed him to do it. Fazal took it as her consent. He stopped the car on the side of a deserted road and turned towards her.

Reena asked, "What happened? Why did you stop the caaa…" Fazal put his finger on her lips to stop her from uttering any more words. She looked at him and saw a kind of fondness in his eyes. He tried to come closer to her. And at last, their lips met. His hand was running over her neck. From the scruff of the neck, his hand came over her bare shoulder… and then shifted to her back. He tried to slide his hand inside her top when she stopped him and tried to get out of his clutches.

"What are you doing?" she asked and adjusted her clothes.

Fazal regained his sense and wondered, "Oh! I am sorry." Then after a pause, he said again, "You are looking irresistible in this orange top. It's not my fault, the culprit is this hot top of yours," and he gave her a naughty smile.

In some time, they reached the hotel. The manager led them to a private dining area.

At the table, Reena threw her deal before him. For a moment, Fazal was stunned. Was she joking or what? Reena repeated her sentence again in a low voice. "Will you play for me? I can pay you Rs 85 lakhs for it."

Fazal was listening with his mouth open. "I can't believe you. I thought I had taken you on a date!" he uttered.

"It will be a great date for you. You have to do nothing for all that money. You have to give up early, that's it," she gave him a sly smile and said.

"What if I say no to you?" Fazal spoke in a serious tone. He had figured out that she was making a fool of him; only he was obsessed with her. Her ulterior motive behind getting close to him was this.

"You can't. You also know many players are doing it and earning quite well, why not you? You are also a human being. Plus, time changes; if it passes away you can't get it back. So it's the time to earn more and more for your future," Reena tried to hit the nail on the head.

"I also want you to talk to Vivek Mishra and Donald Steve about this," she said after a pause.

"I can assure you of my performance, but you will have to talk to them individually. I could just help you meet them," Fazal said.

After having lunch, they came back to the hotel. Fazal called Vivek and Steve to Reena's room and introduced them to Reena. Soon, he left the room with some excuse.

Reena prepared drinks for both and threw the deal in front of them. "I have a great deal for you; you can earn eighty-five lakhs if you do as I say!"

"What do you mean?" Steve asked, turning his face to her.

Reena lit a cigarette and came close to Steve. She sat on the arm rest of his chair, puffed hard and spoke, "Steve, my dear, you just have to give fourteen runs in an over. It could be any over of your choice. And Vivek, you have to make below twenty."

Steve was firm. "Are you crazy? What are you talking about? We don't need to cheat our team," he said.

Reena puffed out a cloud of smoke and laughed. "Oh, you don't cheat! Ha ha ha!" And suddenly became serious, "Who are you fooling? Which match is not fixed? Cricket has become a money game. Everyone is involved in making more and more money. Organisers, sponsors, team owners, all are interested in making a lot of money. Players are paid just a little of that. This time, I brought this opportunity for you guys. If you won't do it, someone else will. Your sacrifice won't be counted, but you will miss the chance."

Vivek disagreed with her. "I don't trust you. I don't know you. Who are you doing this for? Who is behind you?" he enquired.

Reena stood up from the chair's arm rest and went near Vivek. She bent low and sipped vodka out of the glass in his hand. She tried to seduce Vivek. "It would be better that you 'mind your own beeswax' rather investigating my business. You can take my offer or reject it, that's your choice. But do you know that your captain is on my side? Now, think about my proposal; I give you tonight. Tomorrow morning, we will talk again," she said seductively.

Vivek kept his glass aside. He was frustrated with her cheap seductive moves. "You don't have to wait all night. I am not doing this, so don't waste my time and yours."

As soon as he turned to the door, Reena held his hand and said in the same seductive way, "You are not being nice to me."

Vivek looked at her harshly and left the room. Steve also followed him. Both went to Fazal's room. He had just taken a shower and was in a towel.

"Do you know what was happening in there?" Vivek said, annoyed.

Fazal looked at him from the corner of his eyes, and silently searched for his clothes in the wardrobe.

"She said you are already on her side. What does that mean? Do you have any deal with her?" Steve inquired.

Fazal gave him a look and asked, "What have you guys decided?" He went inside to put his clothes on.

"We can't trust her. We don't know who she is. What if she is involved with some kind of sting operation? We don't need to get into all this," Vivek said a little louder.

Fazal came back and said, "I don't think so. She is a fixer for sure. Yes, she has given me an offer also. And I thought a lot. We could take this. We have an opportunity to earn some handsome money. Everyone is earning, why can't we?" He gave them a convincing speech.

"Yeah, you have a point," Steve agreed.

"But I still doubt whether it is safe. For now, I am going to my room. I will see you in the morning," Vivek said and left Fazal's room.

Reena called up Satish and told him that Fazal had agreed but Steve and Vivek had not given her any positive response.

Satish quickly called up Gourav. "Sorry I am disturbing you during business hours. There is something important I have to talk to you about," Satish said.

"Don't be, you can go ahead… I am not that busy right now," Gourav said.

And Satish told everything that had happened between Reena and Vivek.

"Why are you dragging me into all this? It's Vivek's decision, what can I do in this? I don't even know about the deals and all," Gourav said after listening to Satish.

"You have to get into all this…" Satish raised his voice and got impatient. "… because this match is going to be fixed and no confusion will be tolerated. Everything should be clear." He ordered Gourav.

"Do you think he will obey me?" Gourav asked.

"If you guys know who is fixing the match, then he will definitely obey."

"Who is it?" Gourav enquired.

"The underworld don Shakeel Ahmad, he is putting money in it."

Gourav was stunned on hearing the name. He asked in a cracked voice, "Aaare you suuurre?"

Satish sniffed out his nervousness. He said, "Yes, my dear. Reena is the fixer sent by him. So call Vivek and tell him to go through with the offer. And you do it right now. I hope you got it." And he ended the call.

Gourav was in great confusion. He was finding it difficult to decide what to do next. How could he tell Vivek about Shakeel Ahmad? What would he think about him? But it was also necessary to let him know about it; otherwise he could get into danger.

Gourav dialled Vivek's secret cell number. Vivek picked up the phone. "Yes brother, how are you?"

"Not good," Gourav uttered nervously. "I have to tell you something; listen carefully. I came to know that Reena Malik works for Shakeel Ahmad – the underworld don, and she has asked some players, including you, for spot fixing. Just accept the offer, don't go against it." He was almost whispering.

"How could you say all this… and how do you know all about it?" Vivek asked suspiciously.

"Will let you know sometime, but do as I say… Bye," Gourav said and hung up.

After keeping down the phone, Gourav thought 'What am I doing? Am I becoming a puppet in other's hand, who dances on someone's direction? Indirectly, I am working for a don! Oh, crap!'

The next morning, Vivek and Steve met Reena and accepted her proposal. Reena told them exactly what to do. Steve said that he would give a sign before bowling for the paid over, which would be tying his shoe laces. Reena told them that they would get their payment after the tournament at their residences in their respective countries. Reena confirmed to Satish and Hussain that all the three players had accepted the deal. Now that her task was accomplished, so she left for Mumbai.

The day the match started. 'Central Tigers' decided to bat first. The team made 118 runs for the loss of 7 wickets. Fazal and Vivek played as they were told.

'East Royal Champions' had an easy target to chase. In the 16th over, Steve came for bowling, and signalled the fixed over. 'East' easily chased the target and won the match.

With this, 'Central Tigers' got out of the tournament and 'East Royal Champions' entered the finals, where they would play against 'Southern Coast Riders'.

After this, Punit Bhatia was on cloud nine. He had full confidence that his team was going to win the finals. He also assured Shakeel Ahmad that they were going to win the trophy; they had the best players in the league.

And as per his expectations, in the finals, 'East Royal Champions' won the match over 'Southern Coast Riders' and got the BPL trophy.

Celebration in Abu Dhabi

Shakeel Ahmad announced a party; all those who were associated with this fixing scandal and had benefitted from it could come together and celebrate.

Pushkar asked Satish to take Gourav for the party; he had played an important role in this success. Satish met Gourav, told him about the party and forced him to join.

Gourav ignored at first, "Let it be, Satish. I have lots of work here. I do not want to close my shop for this, and I am expecting some consignments from my supplier in the next few days. I don't think I will be available for this party."

"It's okay, good that you are focusing on your shop, but I tell you, the party is next week. You have ten days in hand to receive your consignment. And the party is in Abu Dhabi. You also have an opportunity to go with Shalini on a holiday. As I know, after your honeymoon, you haven't taken her anywhere. She would love to be there, just live your life."

"And let me tell you about the parties! Ahh, they are awesome, I must say. Have experience of a high-profile party once, you will thank me. Come on, come with us! Don't bother about the shop too much; your employees are capable of taking care of it for some time," Satish insisted.

"Okay, I'll talk to Shalini and will let you know," Gourav said. He realised he hadn't taken Shalini anywhere after their honeymoon. She always kept herself busy with household works and nursing his mother. He remembered his promise to her parents that he would keep her happy and would give her all happiness in life.

That evening, Gourav talked to Shalini and left the decision to her. She was happy to travel, and the trip was confirmed.

The venue of the party was Shakeel Ahmad's 'Palm Resort'. It was situated on Al Reem Island. Arrangements were made in the resort itself for all the guests.

Satish and Gourav reached there with their wives. Gourav preferred to take a room close to Satish's room. Shalini and Mona were delighted; they expressed their desire to explore the resort. Satish excused himself as he had to meet Pushkar Mehta and some other persons; therefore Mona went along with Gourav and Shalini.

The weather was very pleasant; the slow and mild sea breeze was ruffling their hair. The resort had a nice landscape; colourful flowers and plants added pleasant aroma and charm to the atmosphere. They reached near the swimming pool – some foreigners were sunbathing by the side. On a distance there was a large fountain which was like the cherry on the cake. Shalini was totally mesmerised by the beauty and charm of the resort. After taking a look at the resort, they came back to their room.

Shalini threw her handbag on the bed in excitement and explored the room. Her room had a balcony. She moved the heavy silken curtain from the glass wall and moved the slider gently. The outside scenery was awesome. The ocean could be seen at some distance.

"Gourav, come see this," Shalini screamed in excitement.

Gourav joined her. He held Shalini from behind and rested his chin on her shoulder. "It's lovely, isn't it?"

"Yeah…" she said.

"Are you happy?"

She winked and said happily, "Very much… I am feeling light and weightless and want to fly like a butterfly."

"Is that so? Let me weigh you…" With that, he lifted her in his lap. "I could make you much lighter," he said and took her inside the room.

Shalini was blushing. She looked into Gourav's eyes and mocked, "Your intentions don't seem right."

"Having such a beautiful wife in this romantic place and not getting naughty? I am not that dumb," he said and put her on the bed. He held her hand in his hand and kissed it. She looked tenderly at him with her big bright eyes. Then he kissed her on her eyes and forehead, and locked lips with her. Both melted into each other's arms and spent the rest of their precious time making love.

Shalini met Pushkar Mehta firstly in the dinner hall, when he himself came to their table. Gourav was talking to Shalini when a husky voice interrupted him.

"Good to see you here..."

Gourav turned; Pushkar Mehta was standing beside him with Satish. He stood up in a hurry to greet him, and also introduced Shalini to him.

"Nice to meet you, Shalini." Pushkar shook hands with her and said, "I hope you like being here."

"Yeah, it's a very nice place," she smiled and said.

"Enjoy your time," Pushkar said and moved ahead with Satish.

"Who was he?" Shalini asked Gourav when he left.

Gourav breathed deep in relief. "He is Pushkar Mehta, a big businessman. Satish had made me meet him once."

"Okay. He looks like a big personality. Look at the way he walks, and his voice is so royal. Isn't it?" Shalini spoke while casting her eye on Pushkar. Gourav glared at her once, she defended herself. "I was just describing what I noticed."

Gourav went to the soup counter and brought chicken soup for both of them.

Shalini took some sips of soup and spoke. "We will go to the beach tomorrow. What do you say?"

"Hmm, we could. It's nearby," Gourav said, "We will return by five o'clock. Satish told me that the party will begin from seven."

"Yes, Mona was telling me that this party is very grand, and renowned personalities will come to attend," Shalini said in excitement.

The party hall was in a corner of the resort and surrounded by a beautiful garden. Inside the hall, a huge chandelier was hanging from the roof. The orchestra was arranged followed by a bar. Heaps of foods were arranged on one side and the entire party hall was filled with well-dressed round tables and chairs with golden orange ribbons.

Gourav and Shalini came to the party with Satish and Mona. Shalini had worn a perfect chocolaty evening gown which she had bought in the morning from the city market especially for the night's party. She accessorised her gown with a thin diamond necklace with matching earrings, which her father had gifted at her wedding. Mona had preferred to wear a designer anarkali suit for the evening whereas Gourav and Satish had worn evening suits.

Pushkar Mehta was sitting at a table with his drink, talking to someone. Satish and Gourav went to meet him.They had a formal talk. After some time, Shakeel Ahmad came in with Hussain and others. He cast his eyes all over and sank into a sofa. Pushkar went to meet Shakeel.

Satish told Gourav about Shakeel Ahmad and his henchman Hussain. They also followed Pushkar. On reaching Shakeel, Pushkar touched his feet. Shakeel picked him up and hugged him.

"Come on, Mehta… How are you?"

"Good, bhai… all your blessings," Pushkar said.

"Hmm, any trouble from Guru Rajan again?" Shakeel asked.

"Not yet. I am very thankful to you," Pushkar said.

Then Shakeel turned towards Satish. "And Satish… how are you doing?" Satish quickly touched his feet. "Good, bhai, until we are under your shed, we can't have any problems," he said with a grin on his face.

Pushkar introduced Gourav to Shakeel, "Bhai, meet Gourav. He played an important role in the success of 'East Royal

Champions' in BPL. He was the one who convinced Vivek Mishra and the other players to play on our side." Then he signalled towards Shalini, "And she is his beautiful wife Shalini."

Shakeel shook hands with him and said, "Nice to meet you, Gourav. How are you?"

"It's a pleasure meeting you, sir. I am good," Gourav said.

Next, Shakeel shook hands with Shalini and asked, "How are you doing, Shalini? Hope you like the party?"

Shalini smiled and said, "I am doing fine, thanks! And the party is wonderful!"

"What do you do, Gourav?" Shakeel asked.

"I am in the bookmaking business and am also running my chemist shop."

"That's good. This party is for all those who are a part of our BPL success. So enjoy the party, and celebrate."

With this, Shakeel got up and moved towards the pool-side to meet other guests.

More guests came. For Gourav and Shalini, it was their first experience. They were stunned seeing celebrities from different areas. Gourav asked Satish, "Are they all linked with BPL?"

Satish said, "Yes, most of them. They would have put their money on the matches."

After a pause, he continued, "Gourav, you might know some of them, right? Do you think they are criminals? Of course not… but they are in the party to celebrate. I brought you here in Abu Dhabi to brainwash you. So many people want to be under his shelter. All have their own motive. Think about yourself. You are making three times more money now than you were making previously, aren't you?"

Gourav kept his wine glass on the table and said, "No, Satish, it isn't like that. But we make opinions on the basis of what we have heard through news and media, and through people. Yes, you are right. I have earned tremendous amount of money since I met you, but I am not at peace. Somehow I always feel some kind of threat and pressure."

"It might be because everything is new for you, but as time passes, this type of feeling will vanish. By the way, threats to some extent are good to keep the minions dutiful," Satish winked and laughed.

In between, a waiter had brought some drinks and snacks; orchestra had started playing melodious English and Hindi songs. The party was in full swing. Some celebrities even took to the stage to dance. After some time, Reena Malik came and joined them on-stage.

Gourav kept asking Satish about the guests. Suddenly, his eyes got stuck on someone. He asked Satish, "Isn't he Punit Bhatia, the owner of 'East Royal Champions'?"

"Yes, of course he is Punit Bhatia. I told you before; you cannot imagine how many people are linked with Shakeel bhai. Also, no one has the guts to go against him," Satish said, munching delicious golden fried prawns.

"You know, Satish, sometimes I think about the common people who love cricket and go crazy for it. Boys bunk school, college, even offices and businesses to watch this game. But, people don't know the actual story behind this. They are getting cheated," Gourav spoke in a low voice.

Satish listened to him carefully, and then said sarcastically, "My dear, if you are talking about faith, then I tell you, it is this very faith and craziness of people for cricket that fixing has become so popular. Bookmakers are taking advantage of it by making a fast buck, and players do it to get more bangs for the buck."

"What about the public sentiment?" Gourav asked.

Satish said, "Money makes people self-centred. If you start thinking about all that, then you can't go far with your ethics." He widened his eyes and prodded Gourav's shoulder. "You have to become selfish to some extent, emotions come later. In today's world, the man who is successful is egotistical, and has left emotions behind."

"Yeah, maybe you are right." Gourav was a little convinced.

Satish took another drink and said, "See, I just know one thing and believe in that. Live life king size. Money is money; whether it is white or black… hmm… it will still get us what we want, won't it?"

A sitting duck

Inebriated, they returned to their rooms by 1:30 a.m. Next day, they slept till late; hung over.

In the evening, Shalini and Mona went to the city market. They insisted their husbands to come along, but the hangover turned Gourav and Satish into 'couch potatoes'. Mona drove to the market. They shopped for hours and were busy collecting souvenirs.

When their shopping was done, they started for their hotel. Around five hundred metres ahead, Mona accidently bumped her car into a parked car. The owner of the car was furious. He came out from his car and started shouting at them. Both the ladies also stepped down. Some nearby people gathered around. The ladies were blaming the man for parking his car on the wrong side.

And a battle of nerves started between them. In a few minutes, police also reached, asked them to show their licence. Mona and Shalini didn't have their licence with them. Police asked them for their passport; they said their passport was in the hotel. Both the ladies were taken to the police station.

There, they called up their husbands and informed them about the situation. Gourav and Satish took their passports and also kept some money, if need be. They grabbed a car from the resort and rushed out.

After a ten-minute drive, they reached a place where a car with flat tyres was stuck in the middle of the road. Satish stopped the car; both of them came out to look at what the matter was. Suddenly, four-five men with arms forced Gourav and Satish to get inside a car. For a few seconds, they couldn't make out what was happening, but after some time, they realised that they were in a pickle. Perhaps they were being abducted.

Guru Rajan was another underworld gangster and Shakeel Ahmad's rival. They often got into turf wars on monopoly. The members of the Guru gang were always baying for the blood of S-company members, and thus they kept their eyes on its activities. Guru Rajan was involved in printing fake Indian currency in Nepal. Some time back, the police had raided his work place in Nepal. He had doubts that Shakeel Ahmad was behind that and that only he could have passed that information to the police.

After that, Guru Gang had blocked the hawala transfer of Pushkar Mehta's ten crore rupees in Karachi. On the orders of Shakeel Ahmad, his men in Karachi took action against the hawala agent and Guru Gang associates. And in that turf war, some of the groupies of Guru Gang were shot. After that episode, Pushkar Mehta became an unsavoury person for Guru Rajan.

Guru Rajan wanted to rule over the cricket world, but till Shakeel Ahmad had a firm grip over it, that was a mere dream for him. He had the knowledge of fixing in BPL, and also had information about the success party that was going on in Abu Dhabi at Shakeel's resort. He came to know that Satish Kaushik was Pushkar Mehta's right hand man and had great contacts with players and celebrities; he was the one who licked them into shape. So he planned to take him on his side.

One of his henchmen was keeping his eye on Satish in Abu Dhabi. The abduction was planned. The day his wife came to the city market, they deliberately placed a car in such a way that she would hit the car and a ruckus could be created. The police were none other than the members of Guru Gang, who came in disguise. They wanted Satish to come out of the resort, and that happened when Mona called up Satish to bring her passport.

"Guru bhai has summoned you."

"Guru bhai...?" Satish tried to recollect the name.

"Never heard underworld don Guru Rajan's name?" one of them said in anger.

Gourav and Satish both blanched at the thought of Guru Rajan. Gourav did not know about Satish, but he had heard about Guru Rajan through news channels and newspapers. He could never imagine even in his dreams that some day he would be meeting him. 'What could be worse than being kidnapped by a gangster? But why? And what about Shalini and Mona? Were they also trapped? Why was Guru Rajan interested in them?' So many thoughts were circling in Gourav's mind.

After some time, they reached a place, where they left the car and walked down a path. They entered a house, where Guru Rajan was lying on the couch and his men were sitting around him.

The gun-men brought Satish and Gourav in front of Guru Rajan.

"Who is Satish?" He looked at them and asked.

One of the gun-men pointed at Satish. "Boss, he is Satish."

"And who is he?" Guru Rajan asked about Gourav.

The same gun-man said again, "Boss, he was with him all the time, so we had to take him also."

Another associate who was keeping an eye on them in the resort said, "Boss, his name is Gourav, and he is a bookie. But now-a-days he is working for Pushkar and Satish."

After listening to them, Guru Rajan stood up from his couch and went near them. "So both of you must be wondering why you are here, hmm?" He paused and further continued, "You people have served Shakeel a lot, now I want you to work for me. Use your contacts and relationships in cricket to my advantage, and against Shakeel's."

Gourav and Satish looked at each other in confusion. Satish asked, "We didn't get you."

Guru Rajan grinned, he put his one hand on Satish's shoulder and with the other he creased his shirt and said, "Okay, I'll make myself clear. Next month, a triangular series of one-day cricket is going to be held, right? You people will have to fix games with players on my direction, just as you did till now for Shakeel. This is one side of the coin. Another side is that you'll have to bluff Shakeel." Guru Rajan emphasised each word.

"It'll remain a secret that you both have been mingled with Guru Gang, and will only pretend that you are working for Shakeel. I want to counter his game, he should bear losses now." He scowled.

"Shakeel will kill us," Satish was scared.

Guru Rajan scowled. "Before that, I'll kill you. Just remember, you don't have any option. And just for your knowledge, your wives are in my custody. You have only two choices – either come to my side and accept my conditions. I'll give you protection from Shakeel and his company. Or get lost with your family… The choice is yours."

Satish was scared enough. Fear had captured him completely. He knew the truth of this ugly world. He quickly assured Guru Rajan that they would do as he says. Guru Rajan looked satisfied.

One of his henchmen took both their mobile numbers. They left them on the road from where they had been abducted. Their car was still there on the side of the road.

After getting free, Gourav's patience wore thin. He asked Satish, "What next, Satish? Where have you taken me along? I had never thought even in my dreams that I would be meeting underworld dons. All because of your blessings! I still can't convince myself what exactly I'm doing here in Abu Dhabi. I even curse the day I met you."

"Stop panicking, nothing is going to happen by crying over spilled milk," Satish said in frustration. "I am also in a soup. Guru Rajan is one of the sworn enemies of Shakeel Ahmad. If I dare to disagree with him, he could have shot both of us on the spot.

"Now we have to think carefully. We can't tell anyone about this incident, not even Pushkar. No one is our own in this world.

The important thing is that we have to follow Guru Rajan's commands, because he has eyes on us all the time," he said while driving the car back to the resort.

"I just want to reach home as soon as possible. I just hope Shalini and Mona are fine," Gourav said and took a deep breath.

Both the ladies were in the resort. They were unaware about the fact that they were in the custody of Guru Gang. They told Satish and Gourav that the police had found them innocent in the case and freed them in an hour's time. Neither Satish nor Gourav told them the truth.

Next day, they took a flight to India and reached home.

Rain on the parade

Gourav was busy in his business. But he had lost his peace of mind. Shalini noticed this. Every time she tried to talk to him about it, he used to ignore her. At last she insisted..

"You don't eat properly. And look at yourself, you are looking pale. Since we have returned from Abu Dhabi, I can feel that you are tensed and worried all the time," she said with concern.

"Nothing like that. I am just focusing on work," Gourav said, looking at some papers.

Shalini snatched the file from his hand and kept it back on the table. "Today was my birthday… Did you remember?" she said angrily.

Gourav was shocked, how could he forget her birthday? He put his hand over his mouth in wonder. He went near her and hugged her. "I am so sorry… happy birthday, my dear!"

She freed herself from his clutches and said huffily, "Everyone wished me today, except you. You didn't even notice me today when I dressed up. Everyone complimented me, said that I was looking pretty, except you. The entire day I waited for your wishes, then I thought you must have planned some surprise… but all in vain." Her eyes became moist, she continued, "Mummy jee was interested in knowing what you have gifted me… I lied that you wished me in the morning and gifted me a dress."

Gourav was feeling very embarrassed. He cursed himself for being so irresponsible. He apologised, "I am very sorry. How stupid I am that I didn't notice all that and ruined your day!"

Shalini interrupted him, "I know you are not like that. There must be something which is bothering you for the last few days."

"Nothing serious, I already told you before," Gourav said and tried to change the topic. "Tomorrow, we will go out and buy something special for you. We'll celebrate your birthday."

"If you really want to see me happy, then tell me the truth. Can't you do this for me on my birthday?" she looked into his eyes and said seriously.

This time, Gourav didn't deny her request. He told her the entire story of the abduction incident and Guru Rajan. Shalini was so scared to know the reality.

"I can't believe that all the incidents were already planned in advance. Oh my god! And Guru Rajan wants you and Satish to work for him… nonsense! No, no, you have to come out from this mess. Leave this bookmaking and all, and stay out of it. Also, try to keep some distance from Satish. You can't be like him…" she was murmuring in nervousness.

"I also want to keep my nose out of this, but now it is not easy. I badly miss my friends. They warned me lots of times, but I didn't listen to them," Gourav bemoaned.

Shalini squeezed his hands gently and rested her head on his shoulder.

❖

ACSU had smelled a rat in BPL. They had information that Reena Malik had some deals with players, thus the team was secretly investigating all the aspects. They had also got information through a whistle-blower that Punit Bhatia had got funds from S-company for his team 'East Royal Champions'. He had pledged to give each player a bungalow in Dubai, and it came to light that those bungalows were in the possession of S-company. With the help of Chennai police, ACSU officers started their investigation from Taj hotel. They got some evidence that she was frequently meeting Fazal Mahmood, so he was the first suspect. The ACSU officer, retired police commissioner R.K. Batra, had called Reena Malik for further investigation. Reena had totally denied making any deals regarding cricket with Fazal Mahmood. She described Fazal as an admirer of hers, and a friend. She also told him that she was a fan of 'Central Tigers' team, that's why she was very enthusiastic that she was staying in the same hotel where the team had stayed, and wished to meet the players. She was very disappointed that the team had lost the match.

The commissioner showed her CCTV footage of the day when she had met Fazal, Vivek and Donald in her room. He asked Reena to say something about that footage. Reena said that they all became friends, and it was a friendly get-together. But she was unable to prove her statements in the interrogation.

All the three players became fixing suspects. Teams of two officers were sent to New Zealand and Pakistan to further interrogate Donald Steve and Fazal Mahmood. And R.K. Batra wanted to meet to Vivek Mishra, himself.

By the time officers reached them, the players had already got threats from S-company to not reveal anything to the police.

Hence, the players described the same things that Reena Malik had said.

The commissioner didn't have any evidence against them, so fixing could not be proved. But ACSU and intelligence agencies were keeping their eye on players. They were linking all the clues so that they could get a clear picture.

The triangular series was close. Guru Rajan made a call to Satish and asked him to inform him if Shakeel had made any strategy of fixing in the coming series. Satish told him that he hadn't got any instructions from Pushkar or Shakeel.

Next day, Guru Rajan called him up again and told him about his own strategy. "I want that Amit Yogi does not take any wickets in the match between India and South Africa, Vivek Mishra does not cross thirty runs and Sunil Choudhary gives sixteen runs in his fourth over. Rs 58 lakhs to each…"

"Okay, I will try to quote this to the players," Satish said.

"If you come to know about any plan of Shakeel's, let me know. I will pay you double," Guru Rajan said and ended the call.

Shakeel was aware that police has an eye on fixing this time, so he chickened out. He already had earned a lot in BPL, therefore had no desire to sail close to the wind. He was focusing on smuggling. And he didn't want to do anything that would cause the police to start noticing him.

Satish reached Gourav's shop, and let him know about the conversation between him and Guru Rajan.

"So Gourav, this is the deal from his side, talk to the players now," Satish said slowly.

"Why don't you talk to them yourself?" Gourav said while writing down something in a register.

"Vivek only deals with you. If you want, I can talk to Amit and Sunil, there is no problem. But I know you can deal with both of them also," Satish said calmly.

"I want to stay out of it now," Gourav said without making eye contact.

Satish became annoyed this time. "Could you stay out of Guru Gang? Remember, it would not be in your favour to disobey Guru Rajan's order. You were also there with me, don't forget. Better to do whatever he wants. It would be good for both of us," he said and left the place.

Gourav flung the register in a corner in disappointment and covered his face with his hands. He didn't want to get into all that, but he was left with no other option than to talk to Vivek.

The cricket series was in South Africa, and the Indian team was flying from Mumbai to South Africa. The entire team was in Mumbai for two days. Gourav called up Vivek, asking to meet him. Vivek told him that it was not possible to meet personally because they had a busy schedule; they could talk over phone only. Gourav told him about the deal, and also requested him to explain to Amit and Sunil for fixing the game. Vivek told him that ACSU had an eye on fixing. So this time, it could be risky. But Gourav insisted and expressed his desire to meet him in Mumbai, so that he could explain everything to him. At last Vivek agreed and let him know the place where they could meet.

Gourav took a flight and reached Mumbai. He was waiting for Vivek. After an hour, Vivek came.

"Do you know the police already suspect me for spot-fixing in BPL, and you want me to take another risk?" Vivek grumbled.

"This deal is not from my side, actually. This deal is from Guru Rajan, and he wants to fix the game," Gourav looked at Vivek for a second and suddenly shifted his eyes away to avoid eye contact with him.

Vivek was shocked to hear that. "Are you insane, how come you take deals from underworld dons? Last time also, in BPL, you told me that that deal was from Shakeel Ahmad. How did you get connected to them?" he grumbled again.

"It's all my misfortune. I want to get rid of this fixing and bookmaking business now, but somehow I am trapped in this. These are underworld names to whom no one could say no. And now only you can help me," Gourav pleaded.

Vivek's eyes were on Gourav. He spoke in disappointment without blinking his eyes. "I used to listen to you because I trusted you. I believed that I won't be getting into trouble because of you. But see, things have changed. Instead of your own deals, you are bringing deals from the underworld to me. And you also want me to involve other players in this… What the crap! Why should I do this?" his voice grew louder.

"I am also doing this unwillingly. I told you, I'm not left with any option," Gourav pleaded.

Vivek thought for some time and said, "Just because I care for you. I will let you meet Amit and Sunil tomorrow morning. Come to the park in front of our hotel. But try to stop all this; otherwise I won't listen to you the next time."

Next morning, Gourav reached the park where Vivek, Amit and Sunil were jogging and doing some exercise.

Gourav let them know about the deals, and they agreed.

Vivek's cell phone was being tapped, and the conversation between Gourav and Vivek was recorded. ACSU officers were tracking every activity of Vivek Mishra. One of the officers recognised Gourav when he came to meet Vivek in the hotel. It became clear to them that Gourav was a fixer and Vivek was involved with him in spot-fixing. Amit Yogi and Sunil Choudhary also got trapped in that.

In South Africa, R.K. Batra called a special meeting with those players. He made them listen to the tape. That tape scared the shit out of them.

"This is a false tape, it's not my voice at all," Vivek screamed in shock.

Mr Batra was sitting on the other side of table. He leaned over the table and said harshly, "I have strong evidence against you, so don't try to mislead me. Now, could you please throw some light on this shit? How long have you guys been involved in spot fixing?" His voice echoed in the room.

"Sir, you might have some confusion, we are not into all this," Amit said.

"Yes sir, it could be someone's strategy to defame us," Sunil also said after Amit.

Mr Batra got up from his chair, came to Vivek and put his hand on his shoulder and asked calmly, "Who was the person on the other side of the phone?"

Vivek's face became pale, but somehow he managed to say, "I don't know."

Mr Batra turned towards his chair, while walking he said, "Come on, don't tell me this, and don't try to escape from my questions." He sat on his chair. "I'll tell you for your knowledge that we had doubts about you, beforehand. Your phone was being tapped on my orders. You also know the validity of the tape, don't you? If this tape comes out from the ACSU, your career would be gone."

After a pause, he continued, "Personally, I don't want to reveal this issue publicly at this moment. It is a matter of dignity for our country. I want you guys to play a genuine game this time. Play for your country and your countrymen. If you do this, it could help you.

"Young blood wants to have everything done quickly. Even earning money! So tell me, Vivek Mishra, who was the person you were talking to?" He looked into Vivek's eyes.

Vivek broke into a cold sweat. Mr Batra had enough reasons and evidence in his hand. His sharp glare seemed to be reading his mind, and was alert enough to catch another lie. He thought that it was better to let him know the truth, hiding facts had no use. So he said, "Sir, his name is Gourav, and he is my cousin. But he is just a go-between guy; actually, the man behind this deal is Guru Rajan. Sir, now you can understand our dilemma as to why it was difficult for us to say no to this deal. Gourav was also left with no other option but to make a deal with us," Vivek defended him.

Mr Batra's pondered deeply, "I see, it's Guru Rajan. And if I am not wrong, semi-finals were also fixed in BPL, right? Who was behind that?" he inquired.

"Sir, it was S-company," Vivek said.

Amit Yogi and Sunil Choudhary, who were unaware of the fact, looked at each other in amazement.

Mr Batra scowled. "I had doubts from the very beginning, I am not surprised, not at all." Then he walked around the table and moved his hand in the air, "I don't know whether the cricket board is scheduling matches for these gangsters or what? It's very unfortunate..." He shook his head vigorously in disappointment. I can't understand why you don't come to us with your complaints and problems? Is it because you are getting a lucrative amount in return for your small favour to them?" he bawled, then he turned towards Vivek and said, "Mr Vivek, you are coming to my office room. I will ask you more questions there. Mr Amit and Mr Sunil, you will also get a call from me later," and he left the room suddenly.

Vivek went after him to the office. Mr Batra asked him to sit and placed a voice recorder on the table, and himself sat across him.

"Now tell me everything in detail. You could start with the BPL semi-finals," he commanded.

Vivek confessed, "Sir, it was the actress Reena Malik who laid the proposal before us." Vivek narrated the entire incident about the deals and the involvement of Shakeel Ahmed.

After listening to the entire story Mr Batra said, "And how much is the Guru gang going to pay you?" Mr Batra asked.

"Rs 58 lakhs," Vivek said.

Batra laughed and said tongue-in-cheek, "Great! You guys earned pretty well for your fear, ha, ha, ha. How much more fixing was there in BPL?" he asked.

Vivek hung his head, "That I don't know. I was only involved in the semi-finals," he said with a hangdog expression.

"Tell me about Gourav, what does he do, and how is he linked with gangsters?" Mr Batra asked.

"That I don't know sir. But he runs his chemist shop, and is also involved in bookmaking."

Mr Batra said, "Hmm, I see. Okay, you may go now. But remember, play a fair game in this series. I am giving you a chance to prove yourself."

Vivek nodded and shook hands with the commissioner and walked out. Mr Batra collected his voice recorder and made a phone call to his office in Delhi. He told an officer to arrest Gourav for interrogation as he was a key suspect in this fixing scandal.

Vivek somehow managed to write a mail to Gourav as his phone was being tapped. In his mail, he informed Gourav about his interrogation and that they wouldn't be able to play as per the deal. He also warned him that officers might come to him for investigation.

Gourav went through the mail and immediately called up Satish. "ACSU has figured out the fixing in BPL and in the coming series also. Vivek has been trapped by an ACSU officer. And any time they can come to me for further interrogation. What I should do now, you tell me?" he asked in a cold sweat.

"But how come they know about that?" Satish asked.

"Vivek's phone was being tapped, maybe."

"Oh shit! Don't worry, give me some time, I'll get back to you," Satish told him.

Satish called up Pushkar and told him everything.

Satish didn't tell him about the fixing in the South Africa triangular series, as he didn't want Pushkar to know about his link with Guru Rajan.

"If ACSU and police reach Gourav, we will get into trouble. Gourav can't take the pressure, I know him, he could reveal our names," Satish told Pushkar.

"Send him underground," Pushkar said. "You can use my Faridabad farmhouse for the house arrest."

Satish again called up Gourav and asked him to reach his house as soon as possible, and not to tell anyone about that, not even Shalini and his parents.

Gourav was confused, but he did as he was instructed. He shut down the shop and called up Shalini to say that he was coming home in two-three hours as he had some important work, and went to Satish's house.

"Why did you call me so urgently?" Gourav asked Satish.

"You have to go underground for some time," Satish said.

"Why should I?" Gourav asked in amazement.

"Because the police and ACSU have set their eyes on you, and any time they can reach you," Satish said.

"It doesn't sound convincing. I have my family, what will I tell them? And moreover, they will get into trouble. Every day, the police will reach my place and will give them trouble by questioning them." Gourav said.

"Don't be panic-stricken; think carefully, this is the only way. You will be safe at Pushkar's Faridabad farmhouse," Satish said.

"No, Satish, I don't agree. I am not a criminal who will stay underground. I accept that I have made mistakes; I was involved in some illegal activities. But now I have made up my mind, I will go with the truth. Doesn't matter whatever it costs, I am ready to pay for it. Now no one can change my mind." There was firmness in Gourav's voice.

Satish thought it was futile to argue with Gourav, he had already made up his mind. He became dodgy – the police could reach him through Gourav in this case. He had to use his muscle power to stop Gourav. Suddenly, four men came and grabbed Gourav from behind. Satish ordered them to take him to Pushkar's farmhouse in Faridabad.

Gourav was stunned.

"I am sorry, Gourav, but you left me with no other option," Satish said and took away his mobile from him.

His men forced Gourav inside the car, and drove to Faridabad.

Evidence doesn't lie

Shalini was waiting for Gourav for dinner. She tried calling him several times, but his mobile was switched off. She started calling everyone she knew. She also called up Satish to check whether Gourav was with him. Satish lied through his teeth and said that he didn't come to him, and they had not even talked to each other for the last few days.

Gourav didn't come that night; Shalini waited for him all night long. Next morning, she told his parents. His father tried his suppliers, clients, and the other shopkeepers nearby, but all in vain. Shalini and her mother-in-law were sitting in their drawing room when the door bell rang. Shalini went to the door. To her dismay, three men were standing there, two in police uniforms, and one in a white shirt and black pants, like an officer.

"Is this the house of Mr Gourav," the officer in the white shirt asked.

"Y…e…s," somehow Shalini managed to utter.

"We have to meet him regarding an inquiry," the officer said.

"Inquiry? In what context?" she asked.

"Could you please call him, we want to talk to him personally."

"He is not at home."

"Where is he then? We visited his shop, it was closed," the officer said.

"Even I don't know where he is. He hasn't come home since last night. Yesterday evening, he called me up and said that he would be coming in a few hours, something urgent had come up, but he didn't come. We are doing everything to trace him, but we don't have any information as yet."

"Oh. So have you registered missing person's complaint at the police station?"

"Not yet," she told him.

"Hmm... If you don't mind, I would like to search your house. Here is the search warrant," the officer showed her the official paper.

Shalini looked at the paper strangely and asked, "Will you please tell me what the matter is?"

"We have information that Gourav is involved in match-fixing scandals," the officer said and entered the house.

Both police officers began searching the house. Meanwhile, the ACSU officer asked Shalini to answer some questions.

"Miss Shalini, you must have an idea what could be that urgent work for which Gourav went," the officer asked.

"He didn't tell me about that. I really have no idea."

"Has it happened before, that he didn't come home for one or two days without informing anyone?"

"No, he always informed me about his whereabouts. It is the first time that he didn't call me up and his phone is also switched off," she said.

"What is his source of income?"

"He owns a chemist shop."

"Apart from the shop, what are the other sources?" he emphasised.

This time, Shalini looked at his face, like she wanted to read his mind. Should she reveal his secrets to the officer? Maybe they already knew about that and just wanted to hear it from her. She said, "He is also a bookmaker."

"Then you must know that he is involved in match-fixing scandals," he said with a smile.

"How can you say that? There are several bookmakers working in this country. Are they all involved in match-fixing? Do you have any proof for your allegation?" She scowled.

"Sir, we got this laptop and two mobile phones from the study room, and we also got some tickets and hotel bills from the drawer." The police officer came out of the room and showed them to him.

"Okay, take them along," and he turned towards Shalini. "Madam, we don't talk shit; ACSU works with evidence. We are taking these things with us and very soon, will summon you to our office for investigation," the officer said and they left the house.

Gourav had been taken to the farmhouse. Few men were already in the house, some of them were armed with pistols. This was the same farmhouse where he had come with Satish to meet Pushkar Mehta.

It was a well-furnished house with all the amenities. Gourav was detained in a room which had a bed, an LCD television and an attached bathroom. To the right of the bed, there was a large window which was covered by a heavy curtain. On the left side, there was a table and chair. After every hour, someone would come in to give him food or water or just to check that everything was all right.

Gourav was annoyed at his vulnerability. One of the men entered the room and gave a phone to Gourav. It was Satish on the line.

Satish said, "I hope you will be all right there. I told my men to take good care of you. You won't have any problems there. I know you must be cursing me in your heart, but it was essential to hide you for some time, otherwise we all could get into trouble because of you."

"For how long will I have to live like this?" Gourav asked in disappointment.

"Till everything settles down, and the police take their eyes off you," Satish said.

"Can I speak to Shalini? She must be worried about me," Gourav said.

"You don't worry. I already told her that you are out of the city for some business, and will come back in ten-fifteen days," Satish lied to Gourav.

Two day had passed. Gourav was still confined to the room. He wanted to talk to his parents, his friends and Shalini; wanted to apologise for his mistakes. So he started writing letters to everyone and he poured all the things which were in his heart in his letters.

❖

Meanwhile, R.K. Batra reached Delhi. The officer updated him about Gourav, and showed him his laptop and documents. His laptop contained lots of information of his clients and regarding bets. Then, Mr Batra looked at the documents, which contained flight tickets, hotel bills and some other papers. He looked at the air ticket to Abu Dhabi. "Have you got any hotel bills or itinerary of where he stayed in Abu Dhabi?" he asked his officer.

"We didn't get any bill or itinerary, but we did get a gift hamper on which it's mentioned 'Palm Resort, Abu Dhabi'," the officer said.

"Palm Resort," Mr Batra parroted while trying to recall the name. "Isn't it the same resort where Shakeel Ahmad threw his party last month, according to intelligence?"

"Yes sir, you are right," the officer said while checking the record file, "The timing corresponds with that of the ticket."

"Hmm... all clues are matching each other. We have to get Gourav. We can get clues about Shakeel from him. Let's summon his wife to the bureau," Mr Batra said.

Shalini was summoned to the ACSU office. She was sitting in front of Mr Batra for interrogation.

"Miss Shalini, I am sorry to be troubling you at this time, but it was important to talk to you as Gourav is missing. Only you can help us in our investigation. I would request you to give your full support; kindly let me know whatever you know. We might get clues to where your husband is," Mr Batra said politely.

"So... Your husband has been in the bookmaking business for quite long. You know that, don't you?" he asked.

"Yes, I knew this even before my marriage; he told me that he entered in this line because he needed money," she said.

"What is the relationship between your husband and Vivek Mishra?"

"Vivek Mishra is my husband's cousin, and moreover, they are like friends."

"Gourav is a bookie, and Vivek is in the cricket team. Moreover, they are friends, close to each other. So there must be some equation between them?" Mr Batra asked.

"I understand what you mean, but I have never asked him about that, and I never had any interest in his work. I have met Vivek only twice till date."

"Recently you visited Abu Dhabi with him; we found air tickets in your house!"

"Yes, we went on a holiday with our friends."

"Hmm… For a holiday or to attend a gangster's party?"

"I didn't get you," she stammered.

"Ms Shalini, we have exact information that Gourav is involved in match-fixing scandals and has links with gangsters like Shakeel Ahmad and Guru Rajan."

"He is not linked with the underworld; it is a false allegation," she cried.

"But Vivek Mishra himself told us that he is connected with the underworld somehow. If not, then what were you doing in the same resort at the same time when Shakeel's party was on at Abu Dhabi?" Mr Batra grumbled.

Shalini was tongue-tied for a while.

"We also have evidence of his involvement in fixing matches in the current cricket series in South Africa," Mr Batra said. "This time, he has taken deals from Guru Rajan. Could you please throw some light on it?"

Shalini replied in a conciliatory voice, "Actually, the thing is not what it seems..."and Shalini let Mr Batra know about the whole incident and the conditions which were imposed by Guru Rajan on them.

"Oh! I see," Mr Batra exclaimed. "And what was behind the spot-fixing in the BPL semi-finals?

"Sir, I don't know about that in detail, but I remember that just a day before the match, Satish called up Gourav. I didn't hear their conversation but noticed that somehow, he was not looking convinced while talking to him. And just after that, Gourav called up Vivek. He was very disturbed for a few days. I don't know whether it was related to the semi-finals fixing or bookmaking," she said.

"Do you know where Satish lives?"

"Yes, I do." Shalini nodded.

"Okay, you can tell the address to my officer. Thank you so much for your support. I hope your husband is found soon," saying that, Mr Batra left the room. His next strategy was to trap Satish, and to find out how the chain works.

Slaughter

In South Africa, the match was on between India and South Africa. Guru Rajan was expecting to earn handsome money in this match. On the other side, Satish was trying hard to get the deal final with the players. He contacted two or three fixers there to reach the players and get the deal done, but security was tight and they couldn't make it till the last moment.

South Africa batted first and scored 278 runs. All the Indian players played their own game. That burst Guru Rajan's bubble; nothing was happening according to the deals. He called up Satish thrice, but his mobile was switched off. Satish deliberately did it. He knew that he could not face Guru Rajan; he wouldn't listen to any excuses. He was planning to fly away somewhere for some time.

Guru Rajan's anger flared up more when he couldn't get connected to Satish. He growled in anger, "I know he must have changed the deal, that son of a bitch! How dare he cheat me, the bloody ass-licker of Pushkar! Making a mockery of me by switching his mobile off, the swine! Drag him in front of me, I will let him know what happens to people who flout my orders," he said, piqued.

His henchman was in Mumbai. On his command, he reached Delhi with his gang. Keeping an eye on Satish's activity, they made out in no time that he was planning to flee the city, as he was meeting with travel agents, visiting his bank and meeting some hawala agents.

One night around 10 p.m., when Satish was returning home, after taking tickets to Singapore from his travel agent, the Guru Gang members started following him. Satish was driving his car; lost in thoughts. There were so many things running in Satish's mind at that time that he didn't notice that a car was following him.

He stopped at a traffic signal; the car came from the right side of Satish's car and stopped also. Satish glanced at them; five people were inside the car. He turned his head towards the traffic signal that had become green till then. He drove ahead. He suddenly realised that the same car had been following him from quite a long time. The car sped up and crossed Satish's car. After a distance of nearly 30 metres, the car stopped so as to block the road. Satish put his foot on the brake. All five people came out of their car; four of them had pistols in their hands.

Satish smelled a rat at a glance. He put his car in reverse gear nimbly towards the main road. Seeing he was backing away, the men rushed to their car. They turned their car in the same direction and started chasing him. Satish was driving as fast as he could. He was honking continuously so that other vehicles on the road would move aside quickly. The henchman driving also put his foot down and sped up. After chasing him for three to four kilometres, they started firing at Satish's car. "Let's kill him now, he is trying to escape," the henchman said with anger. Few bullets hit Satish's car, his heart was beating fast, and he was driving recklessly. His car hit some drums arranged by the traffic police on the roadside to slow down speeding vehicles. Satish straightened his car, but the gangster's car came close and they shot straight through the glass on the right side. The glass broke; Satish got some cuts on his hands and face because of the broken glass pieces. That scared the shit out of him. Again he tried to speed up his car, faster and faster. Another bullet punctured the front wheel of the car. Satish was driving at 100 km/hr; he lost control over the car and his car collided with a wall with a big bang. His head smashed against the steering, causing the horn to blare continuously.

A cacophony of bullets firing, the car crash and the horn beep had drawn the attention of folks nearby. A few vehicles stopped on seeing the horrific scene. A police PCR van passing by rushed to the spot. By then, the gang men escaped from the spot.

Police reached the car, and saw that a man was lying on the car's steering wheel. They moved him back on the car seat. His head was smashed. One of the police officers called an ambulance, which came after fifteen minutes. At the hospital, the doctors declared him dead.

Satish's death agitated Pushkar Mehta. 'Who could be behind the attack?' he wondered. 'Guru Rajan? Might be possible, with the rift between us.'

He tried to assess what the involvement of Guru Rajan in the attack would mean. "Either he wants to make me feeble by killing Satish, or it could be a warning for me that I am his next target... does he want to destroy me?" Pushkar was trying to figure out what could be the possible reasons for the Guru Gang to attack.

Mr Batra reached Satish's house with his team and spoke to his wife. There, he came to know that Satish Kaushik had been running at least several illegal bookmaking centres in different cities like Mumbai, Chennai, Delhi and Punjab. Apart from this, he was also active in the real estate business. He was working under Pushkar Mehta's syndicate. Mona was not aware of his business details, but she let them know that Satish had good contacts with many businessmen, players and celebrities.

When asked if she knew her husband was involved in match-fixing, she hung her head and agreed. She also told that recently, they had celebrated a big success at a party in Abu Dhabi.

"Success in what?" Mr Batra asked.

"Everyone had earned a good return in BPL, it was for that... I only know that," Mona said.

"Who had thrown the party?"

Mona stayed mum for a while. "Don't hesitate, your statement will help the police reach the attackers. And we have arranged security for you also. You will get full protection, so don't worry," Mr Batra said.

"Shakeel Ahmad," Mona uttered.

"Shakeel Ahmad," Mr Batra parroted. "Now tell me about the party; who was there, there must have been some known and famous faces. I heard that Shakeel likes to throw grand parties."

Mona described the whole party and named several businessmen, politicians and celebrities, including Punit Bhatia and Reena Malik. Those were the names that had come up earlier in the BPL match fixing scandal through intelligence. Now Mr Batra had evidence against them.

Gourav couldn't believe what he saw and heard over the news channels; he was totally stupefied. He didn't eat anything for a day and more; his throat refused to swallow anything in shock, nervousness and grief.

The armed men at the farmhouse were also confused and directionless. Gourav pleaded them to let him go as Satish was not alive anymore.

Gourav reached home. Everyone was relieved to see him.

He discovered that Satish had lied to him about taking care of his family; he never called up Shalini to inform her. Gourav's heart was filled with disgust. His family had gone through unnecessary distress.

The police was searching for Gourav as per the missing report filed by his father. So after learning that he had reached home, he was arrested and charged for involvement in match-fixing scandals.

❖

Gourav was sitting in front of Mr R.K. Batra during interrogation.

"We know about your involvement in match- or spot-fixing in cricket, so it will be better if you tell us the whole thing," Mr Batra said. He played the tape on which he was talking about the spot-fixing deal with Vivek Mishra.

Gourav told him with composure about the incident that had happened in Abu Dhabi. The abduction… the meeting with Guru Rajan… and the fixing deal.

Mr Batra asked him about his connection to Satish. Gourav told him how he came to be in contact with him.

When asked who could be behind Satish's murder, Gourav named Guru Rajan as a possible suspect.

Mr Batra asked Gourav about the BPL fixing and that of the semi-final between 'Central Tigers' and 'East Royal Champions'.

Gourav told him that he had not been directly involved in this scam, but Satish had pressurised him to talk to Vivek on the matter. Through him, he learned that Shakeel Ahmad was behind that deal and that Pushkar Mehta, Reena Malik and Punit Bhatia were also involved. The success party had been held in Abu Dhabi and several big shots were invited to that.

Never know what's around the corner

On the basis of evidences and statements of Vivek, Mona and Gourav, the committee had charged Reena Malik, Punit Bhatia, Pushkar Mehta, Vivek Mishra, Fazal Mahmood, Donald Steve, Guru Rajan, Shakeel Ahmad, and all the other people whose names came to light. The police was working on collecting evidence against them. They conducted raids and arrested several bookies and punters on the basis of account details found from Satish's office and with Gourav's help.

Police also raided Naseef Ali's bookmaking centres and seized more than hundred cell phones, several laptops, iPods, lot of cash, and account information of clients and bookies. He had used his gadgets to connect Indian bookies with Pakistan via conference calls. Naseef was in Pakistan when the police raid occurred. He came to know from his sources that Gourav had been assisting the police.

News channels were getting one breaking news after another related to fixing scandals.

❖

In Pakistan, Naseef was boiling with anger. Police had issued an arrest warrant against him. He wanted to take revenge on Gourav. He heard about Satish's slaying and tried to call Pushkar on this matter. "Hello Boss! Naseef here."

"Naseef! How are you?" Pushkar said.

"I heard about Satish, it's strange."

"Hmm... but I will figure out that bastard for sure," Pushkar said in disappointment.

"Boss, the police has issued an arrest warrant against me in India; they have seized all my centres and belongings there. And that bastard Gourav, who I helped in his bad days, is passing information to the police. I want to kill him," Naseef said.

"I also have information that he is helping the police by passing information about bookmaking and spot fixings. Maybe he thinks that he will be safe from all allegations against him if he helps ACSU and the police in their investigation. He will pay for this," Pushkar said in anger.

"That's what I am saying, we should finish him. He has made us suffer a lot." Naseef yelled.

"You don't worry, he won't survive much longer," Pushkar said affirmatively.

After their conversation, Pushkar ordered his men in Delhi to finish off Gourav.

❖

As usual, Gourav started winding up his shop around 10 p.m. He walked to his bike in the parking lot.

As he was wearing his helmet, two men on a bike stopped near him. One of them got off the bike briskly and stabbed him several times. Gourav was baffled by this sudden attack. The man driving the bike told his partner to get back on before anyone came around. They drove away, leaving Gourav in a pool of blood. Hearing his screams, some people gathered around, including the parking attendant, who recognised Gourav. An auto driver offered to take him to the hospital. At the hospital, doctors said that he had sustained severe injuries to his abdomen and was in a very critical state.

PART IV

Around 1 a.m., a bang on our door startled me. I switched on the light and checked the time. I opened the door. Papa was standing there with the cordless phone in his hand. He looked sad.

"Papa… What happened?" I asked in alarm.

He handed me the phone. "Call for you."

"Who is it?" I asked.

Papa didn't say anything and turned away after giving me the phone.

"Hello," I uttered.

"Amit… Amit…" It was Rajeev. "Gourav is no more…"

I was stunned, I couldn't believe my ears. Rajeev continued to speak, "Gourav's father called around 11:45 to say that Gourav's condition was getting serious, his organs were failing. Doctors were unable to stop the bleeding and more blood was required. So we were trying to arrange for more blood.

"When I called to ask about his condition a few minutes ago, he told me that he is no more… we have lost him," Rajeev's voice was thick with sorrow.

On hearing this, I drove to the hospital in a rush. Richa insisted on coming with me. My heart was melting. I was in my hometown after a long time to celebrate Diwali with family and friends. I remembered the days when we four celebrated the festival with much fun. I had come to India to relive those days with my friends and whoop it up with our wives also. But who knew that destiny would show us mournful days instead of joy.

I was deep in thought, thinking if Gourav had chosen this for himself. One thing I understood then, that our destiny gives us time to think and choose the correct path; it's we who have to take the decision at the right time, at the right place. Once the time has passed, nothing can be done.

Perhaps Richa understood my mental state. The constant stream of thoughts in my mind came to rest when she squeezed my hand with her soft hands to calm me. I took a deep breath and focused on driving.

We reached the hospital. Gourav's room was shrouded in heart-broken silence. Rajeev, Nitin and Gourav's father were mournfully sitting outside the room. The sound of wailing rose from inside the room at intervals. We went inside. Gourav's mother was sitting near his body and wailing from time to time. Shalini went close to her, choking with tears herself. "It was my time to go. Why has god taken him away…" she lamented.

In the morning, we took his body home. Gradually, people started coming to pay their condolences. The police and media persons also came to cover the news of Gourav's death.

❖

The case was primetime news on all the news channels. Gourav's murder reflected a big criminal threat from underworld, after the slaying of Satish. The police were criticised for failing to giving proper security to a key witness in the entire match-fixing racket. The police was investigating each and every aspect of Gourav's attack, as he had made many enemies by helping ACSU and Delhi Police.

The case became clear when police arrested Naseef Ali. In one of his statements, he revealed that Gourav had been attacked on Pushkar Mehta's orders.

The police issued arrest warrants against Pushkar Mehta, Shakeel Ahmad, Guru Rajan, Reena Malik and others who were involved.

Cases were registered against Vivek Mishra, Amit Yogi and Sunil Choudhary under the Gambling Act and Indian Penal Code section 415, which pertain to cheating and forgery.

Gourav's mother couldn't live with the grief of losing her son and a month later, she also passed away. Now, Shalini and Gourav's father together run 'Gourav Medicals', his dream.

PART V

A new direction to life

One year later

Subhash Modi, Commissioner of BPL, faced continuous life threatening attacks. He nearly escaped shoot-outs in Dubai, Malaysia and Mumbai.

Mr Batra reached Mumbai to meet him at his residence.

One of his staff welcomed Mr Batra. "He's in the shower, you may wait here," he said and showed him up to a grand sitting room.

Fifteen minutes later, Subhash Modi arrived, followed by his butler with a tea-tray. "Good to see you safe, Mr Modi," Mr Batra shook hands with him.

"What is good, Mr Batra? Seeing me in single piece? It was the third attempt on my life. Me and my family don't feel secure anymore?" Modi passed a cup of tea to Mr Batra.

"I understand, Mr Modi. Police and intelligence are working through thick and thin. All the underworld gangsters have been holed up in Middle Eastern countries since the arrest warrant has been issued against them. We also have agents keeping an eye on their different rackets, and that's why every time we have warned you before the attacks, isn't it?"

"For this, I am grateful to you," Modi said tongue in cheek. "I was again threatened last night. They want a fix in BPL matches, or I will be killed. Your information is not surety of my life," Modi's frustration was palpable, his cheeks turned red and wrinkles thickened on the forehead. "You know, people think that I have helped my close ones buy stake in franchises and that I have been involved in match-fixing. But the truth is, I have had three assassination attempts on me for my stand on anti-corruption. Last year I had refused to kowtow to Guru Rajan in his attempts to fix matches in BPL, and came at his gunpoint in Malaysia," Modi's voice pitch was pinning the ear.

He sipped his cup of tea, took a short break and a deep breath. His voice softened, "Thanks to your agency and the local police who rescued me safely," Modi said and shook his head in disappointment.

"Mr Modi, it's not that we are not capable of catching these gangsters, of course we are. But the country and its government have to work under its constitution and the laws. Currently India does not allow operations outside Indian soil," Mr Batra said.

"Currently, we are providing you special security. We have chosen three commandos from Anti-Terrorism Squad. They will work on direct orders from ATS."

"Indian force can't get hold of Guru Rajan or Shakeel, it seems," Modi said coldly and looked up, resting his head on the sofa-back, starring at the hanging chandelier. "I don't see a good future of my family in this country. Irrespective of my contribution in cricket, I am being alleged to corruption. No one understands I am here to clean up the bloody game. Some people even think, I am linked with underworld. I want peace now, for me and for my family. That's why, I have decided, I will leave this land and move out to another country. I am going to resign from my job…"

Shalini was tallying accounts on the laptop; working for long had made her drowsy. She shut the laptop down and went to the kitchen. A cup of ginger tea would boost her energy up. With tea in one hand, she came to living room and switched on the television for the news of the day.

'*Subhash Modi, commissioner of BPL, has resigned. His resignation came after the shootout happened outside his residence in Mumbai.*

Disobeying the demands of the underworld has made his life difficult in the country and he is leaving for London.' Shalini sipped her tea while listening to the news.

Shalini stared at the cup in her hand. She revolved the cup around and kept staring at it. She had bought this mug in Abu Dhabi. It reminded her of that ugly day when the abduction had happened. How everything was pre-planned by Guru Rajan, that accident… the abduction… and the trap.

Suddenly, she remembered something, and put the cup on the table. Once, she had seen something in Gourav's diary. 'Where it could be?' She thought and ran her finger upon the books and files kept in a rack. She shut her eyes, tried hard to retrieve the image of the diary. After a few seconds, she could remember, the diary had a dark green cover on it. She went to the glass wall cabinet. And there she found the diary, standing in a book row, squeezed between two fat marketing books.

In one of the pages, Gourav had tried to mention all of the landmarks he had seen in Abu Dhabi during his abduction, while on the way to Guru Rajan's den.

'The abduction took place on Hazard Bin Zayed St. After ten to fifteen minutes we were on the bridge crossing the sea; then after a gas station on the left side, the vehicle diverted to right on a street which had a small round-about, a leopard kind of animal's statue and a school with a grey-coloured building. We passed through an alley; that had a gym and also a beauty salon, and came up to an unimproved dirt road. At last the road met a street, which had a mosque; the other side of the street had local markets. Then we came up to an urban road, it had tall buildings and skyscrapers. The car took a long 'U' turn, saw Audi's showroom on the side and entered into a street that led us to an avenue, having large shrubs planted along each side. Then, came up to a road, most of the buildings were coloured in yellow, saw a garage there. Then the car entered into a narrow street, both sides of the road had old and antiquated buildings, some of them ready to tumble down. We walked down the path. We crossed through a labyrinth of ancestral pile and reached Guru Rajan's hideout.'

Shalini read the page several times. Something was running inside her mind. She searched Mr Batra's contact number and fixed up a meeting.

❖

"I saw the news of another attack on Subhash Modi. He is leaving the country," Shalini said while looking at Mr Batra. She paused and continued, "Sir, it's been more than a year of Gourav's death, and people like Pushkar, Shakeel and Guru Rajan are still free. Is it too difficult to get hold of them? Or police is waiting until they do something big?"

"Mrs Mishra! They are beyond the country's law and order, hiding somewhere in the neighbouring countries. Their arrest is not a cup of tea. But agencies are doing their work. My work is limited to stopping corruption in cricket. Catching underworld mafia doesn't fall under my work domain. There's another department in the police which takes care of it," said Mr Batra.

"Sir, I have something that can help reaching the criminals. I want to help out the police by giving clues to them." Shalini said in a stern tone.

"What clues? And what do you have?"

"Sir, I have got a diary, in which Gourav has sketched out the location of Guru Rajan's base in Abu Dhabi. Indian Intelligence is looking for some clue; which I might have this time. Also, I want to help the IB in catching these most wanted criminals by working with them."

Mr Batra's eyebrows were raised. "You want to join IB?"

She nodded. "I want to do this for Gourav. And it will give some aim to my life," said Shalini.

"It's not an easy job…"

"Still, I want to get into this," Shalini interrupted Mr Batra in between.

"You should meet Mr Vikram Sood. He is the Joint Director in IB. He is the right person to speak to. I will call him up," said Mr Batra and called up Mr Sood right away. He agreed to meet her up.

Vikram Sood met her in a cafeteria. Shalini showed him the diary and spoke about the Abu Dhabi incident. She also expressed her desire of becoming a part of the operation. Vikram Sood was not comfortable making her a part of any operation, it was not easy, and officers who conducted operations are highly trained. But Shalini was firm. She said she was here to help the police reaching those gangsters who were hiding inside their cave and running their crime syndicates in India. She wanted to help police root out these criminals completely, and was determined to be a part of it. She had some thoughts and clues which could help in an operation against them.

"Why do you want to endanger your life?" Mr Sood asked Shalini.

"This mission gives a new direction to my life and also I want to avenge Gourav's death," she explained.

Vikram looked at Shalini for some time and said that he would call her in sometime; he needed some time to think over it.

At night Shalini received a phone call. Mr Sood had agreed upon Shalini's inclusion in the operation. And she could come from the next day for her special trainings.

Next day, Shalini reported on time. Mr Sood introduced her to other officers and said, "They will train you physically as well as mentally. Your mental strength would be your vital weapon in any circumstances and the other most important aspect is, hiding your own identity, that's your only defence at an operation. Now onwards, your honesty and your life is only and only towards the bureau, not even for your family."

Mr Sood smiled at her and wished her luck. She moved forward for the training.

I'm Game

Five months later...

ABU DHABI, PALM RESORT

The assistant manager of the resort had called up the regular meeting of housekeeping staffs to change their shifts and location.

"Monica, you are assigned to Sapphire, morning shift," the manager said to a lady, and gave a checklist book.

Emotions were running up and high inside Monica after hearing her duty in Sapphire. Sapphire was a section in the resort, having fifty rooms and twenty suites. She pushed the room attendant cart towards Sapphire with a heavy heart but kept a nice plastic smile over her face and was greeting everyone passing by. The corridors of Sapphire were looking familiar to her, even when she had not visited this part of the resort since joining.

She stopped at room number S019, the door had a tag for room cleaning request. She had been here earlier also. She put the MasterCard on the lock and the door opened. She stepped in, her eyes moist. She took a deep breath and looked around. That was the same room where she had stayed with her husband once. She went close to the window and moved the heavy silken curtain aside; the enormous blue sea could be seen at a distance. She happened to slide the glass partition and came out in the balcony. Gently, a cool breeze touched her face; she closed her eyes for a moment. The wonderful memories of this room resurfaced before her eyes.

She remembered the day, the sky was pink with the setting sun, and she was sitting in the balcony with her husband enjoying the exotic wine. The romantic cool breeze from the sea seemed to spray some kind of love essence in the air. She had been so close to him that she could feel his warm breath and heard the sound of his heart. He gently pressed his cold lips against hers and had whispered 'the wine is tastier here'. Then he had scribbled some poem in the nearby corner of the balcony.

Monica opened her eyes and wondered if the poem was still here. Her curious eyes searched every corner of the wall. At last she found the writing hidden behind a thin layer of dust; she wiped the wall surface. Now it was visible. She touched the lines while she read through.

You are the sun in my day;
My inspiration,
The wind in my sky;
My love,
The waves in my ocean;
My emotions,
And the beat in my heart;

My life.
I love you.
I love you more
in that I believe,
You had liked me
for my own sake
And for nothing else.
I could never tire of saying,
Shalini, I love you.

She cried aloud; her fate had snatched her happiness and dream she wished with Gourav. Her tears were oozing out. No one was there to console her, except that cool breeze which was still ruffling her hair.

She tried to recover her normal state when she had a call from her father-in-law.

"Hello…"

"Are you all right, Shalini beta?" her father-in-law said.

"Hunh, I am fine. How are you?"

"How I could be, without you? Just waiting for the day you will come back. It's been so long you left. When are you coming back, beta?" he asked.

"My work is incomplete papa. I can't say when, but I will return," she said.

"Where are you? What are you up to?" He sounded curious.

For a while there was complete silence between both of them. Then her father-in-law spoke coldly, "You never speak up about your work; don't know why? But I am always worried for you. Not speaking to you even for a weak makes me restless.

Who else is mine on this earth other than you? What would I do if something happens to you…" he became emotional.

"Nothing would go wrong papa, trust me. You are my strength. I can't see you shattered like this. I will be back soon, but till then, have belief and hope. I am bound not to let anyone know where I am and what I am up to. But have faith in me, and pray for my success. I will never let you down," she stopped for a while then continued ahead, "I will call you up twice a week, promise. Please don't think too much."

Soon she finished the call, went to the washroom and washed her face. She was feeling lighter inside. She looked at herself in the mirror; she found her eyes slightly swollen and hair untidy. She quickly took out her mini make-up kit which she carried every time and gave a fine touch to her face. Now she was looking ready. 'Ready' for the work she was here for. She was on a mission to dig clues about Shakeel Ahmed and his henchmen. And she was sure to get those in Palm Resort only.

She cleaned the room. While arranging the bed, she found an ID card. Mohammad Ajeez. She knew him, and had even met him once. Gourav had introduced him to her. He was a businessman, a cricket buff, also a punter. She remembered Gourav had told her about Mr Ajeez that he was a good man. He keept knowledge of everything related to his business, cricket, underworld's activity or politics.

Mr Ajeez could give her some clues. She should meet him up, she thought. But she couldn't meet him in the palm resort, as it could reveal her identity. Then she made a plan.

❖

In the evening Mr Ajeez received an envelope from the reception counter. He opened the envelope in his room, there was a letter inside;

Dear Mr Ajeez,

I hope you remember me; I am Shalini, Gourav's wife. We had also met before, in Delhi.

I learnt you are staying in Palm Resort. So I wanted to meet you. Can we meet at Cafe Nero tomorrow around 11 a.m.? I will be waiting.

Shalini.

Ajeez thought for some time. He could remember Shalini. But what was she doing in Abu Dhabi? And why did she want meet him now? He decided to meet her up the next day.

Mr Ajeez reached Cafe Nero, found Shalini, already waiting there for him.

"Shalini!"

"Mr Ajeez! Nice to see you here."

Ajeez pulled a chair back and sat facing Shalini.

"How come you are here in Abu Dhabi?" he asked.

"I had some work here. I saw you outside the resort yesterday. I went inside to confirm if it was really you, and left the message. In a foreign place, seeing a known person is such a nice feeling,"Shalini tried to divert Mr Ajeez's question.

Mr Ajeez simply smiled at that. After a short silence he said, "I am sorry for Gourav. Whatever happened was unfortunate.

In this world, it's easier becoming bad, but becoming good demands sacrifices. It is really unfortunate.

"I am quite aware of everything. I warned him earlier, never get close to such people, but unfortunately, he was trapped. These people carry great contacts, whether political, social, law or police. That's why many of them are free to roam, despite an arrest warrant. They have every solution against our country's law. It's not easy to get hold of them. See, Pushkar Mehta is moving freely on bail and after sometime, he would be completely free in the name of lack of evidence against him." Saying that Mr Ajeez boggled and asked Shalini, "You didn't tell me, what you are doing here?"

Shalini didn't say anything.

"Don't say you are here for Pushkar Mehta?" Mr Ajeez said out loud.

Shalini was mum again. Mr Ajeez understood her silence, "Oh no! You came all the way to look for Pushkar Mehta? It's insane. It's not a cup of tea Shalini! Go back home."

"Mr Ajeez, I called you here with a hope, that you can help me out. I know you are different. Though you have to deal with some gangsters off and on and you meet them for your business purposes, but I know you don't admire them. You dislike them just as much as me. Please let me know if you know about Pushkar or Shakeel. Do you know where they are?"

Mr Ajeez looked at her carefully and said, "Shalini! What are you up to? What is going inside your mind? You want to avenge your husband's murder? How? Do you think you can kill Pushkar, if he comes in front of you? It will just be a one-sided game in which you will suffer, not him. Every time he is surrounded with his henchmen. You are risking your life. Take my advice and return."

"Now it's been the aim of my life, Mr Ajeez. Doesn't matter how much time it takes, but I am sure I will find out Gourav's murderer someday. My revenge is my life. I can't step back now."

Ajeez saw Shalini, her gesture was confident and voice was firm. She looked determined and fearless.

"I heard, Pushkar will be in Malaysia next month," Mr Ajeez said.

"In Malaysia? When and Where?" Shalini asked.

"That I don't know. But I know someone who can give you this information. His name is 'Sunny Baweja'; he looks after Pushkar's gems and jewellery business in Dubai. Right now he is in Palm Resort for four days."

"Thanks Mr Ajeez, it's a great help."

"I can just wish you luck," Mr Ajeez said and left.

Sunny Baweja was in a bath robe, standing in front of the mirror, busy shaving when the door bell rang. He peeped out through the partially opened door.

"Room service sir. Any laundry?" The staff asked.

Sunny let him inside, "There on the desk, collect all," he signalled and went inside the washroom.

The staff came inside. He slowly locked the main door from inside, covered his own nose and mouth with a cloth and entered the washroom. Before Sunny could sense out something, he sprayed some gas over his face. Sunny fainted in no time.

The staff dragged him to the room, tied his feet and hands, and left him on the floor. Then he searched the room and his belongings until Sunny recovered.

"Who are you?" Sunny asked in amazement.

"Let it be, doesn't matter. Just answer me."

"What nonsense! Why should I answer you? Leave me, otherwise I will scream."

The man took out his gun and stuffed it inside Sunny's mouth, "In no time, I can finish you off. So just answer me whatever I ask without any question," he said sternly.

The gun in his mouth made Sunny shiver and quiver, he looked into the stranger's stoned eyes, and no mercy could be seen. He was breathing very fast and felt dizzy.

The stranger took out the gun from his mouth and asked, "What do you know about Shakeel, where is he?"

"I have no idea about Shakeel. I met him twice only, once in this resort and next in Dubai, eight months back. I don't know where he isnow," Sunny said and breathed.

"And Pushkar Mehta, where will he be found?"

"I just know he would be attending an event in Malaysia next month on the seventeenth in Four Seasons Resort, Langkawi."

"Are you sure about this?" the stranger asked.

"Yes, he told me. He would be meeting some businessmen there and would invest in their business."

The stranger stood up and warned him, "If the information proves wrong, you would be finished with your family. Just pray no further change in Pushkar Mehta's program. Otherwise you will have to pay the cost." He freed his one hand and left the room.

Sunny was still in shock, couldn't apprehend whether to acknowledge the incident to Pushkar or not. And finally he decided to keep mum over it.

❖

Shalini took a swift right turn towards the staff room. After some distance, she turned back to recheck if anyone was following her. No one was there. She quickly entered into a room and closed the door. The man in the room was dumping his belongings into a backpack and turned to look up at her.

"Did he give you the location of Pushkar or Shakeel?" Shalini asked.

"He doesn't know about Shakeel. But Pushkar would be in Four Seasons Resort Langkawi on seventeenth, next month in Malaysia, he told me," the man said and put his gun in the backpack along with other stuff.

She walked towards him. Her eyes refused to take off from him for even a moment.

"Why are you packing the stuff, sir?" Shalini asked amazed.

"I am leaving this place. After threatening Sunny Baweja, this is the first thing I should do. You have to manage here on your own. We finally dug out Guru Rajan's base; the location sketch you provided has helped a lot. Now the action time has come. In sometime we will go live on the video call with our chief, Mr Rathi," saying that, he took out his laptop and placed on the table. He sat in front of the camera and signalled Shalini to sit beside him.

Shalini came and sat next to him. The video call was on. Mr Deepak Rathi was the Additional Secretary of Research and Analysis Wing (RAW) and the chief of the operation was online.

"How's it going there Arjun? What's the update?" Mr Rathi asked the senior most officer Arjun Singh.

"Sir! We have discovered Guru Rajan's base. To know more about his nest, Govind has been placed there as a liquor supplier. He will provide us the clear picture of his base, after that we can make our plan accordingly," said Arjun.

"That's great, we are trying to catch Guru Rajan for a long time. Every time he slips out with a short margin. If you are sure it's him, then be extra careful, this time he shouldn't slip out."

"Sure sir! We have information that around seventeen to twenty henchmen are always there at a time.They also possess good amount of weapons. So we need four more officers here."

"Hmm, I have to talk to the Director first and further to the Home ministry. We need their approval for further action," Mr Rathi said.

"Sir! I beg to differ, but approvals from ministry take time. In the past also, we have missed some cases because we were waiting for orders..This time we are very close to catch Guru Rajan and if he manages to run, then not only will it be our biggest failure but it would be impossible to reach him the next time," Arjun disagreed with Mr Rathi.

Mr Rathi understood his concern and said, "You are not wrong, Arjun! But this time, things are different. We have a new government. And sometime back only, a treaty has been signed between both the nations. I hope Abu Dhabi government would show its supportive side."

"Sir! We have one more lead of Pushkar Mehta. Next month's seventeenth, he is in Malaysia. Through him we can reach Shakeel Ahmed," said Arjun.

"How sure are you that Pushkar has information about Shakeel?" asked Mr Rathi.

"Sir! I know him," said Shalini. "Shakeel is like his guru and mentor, and an incitement behind his every illegal business. He is attached to Shakeel with his roots. We must trace Pushkar for Shakeel."

"Hmm...," Mr Rathi was thinking rationally, when Arjun interrupted, "Sir! He would be there for some business dealing. So it might be a short trip. We need to do things quickly in that case. In my opinion, Shalini should go there. She has an advantage of seeing and meeting him in person in the past. It would help recognising him, if he comes in disguise," said Arjun.

"Hmm, Shalini! Pushkar is not just a refugee or a clue to reach Shakeel, but also the murderer of your husband. You would need to hold back your anger and revenge against him and work with your intelligence. Do you think you can do it with full responsibility?"

"Sir, I could never forget that he is my culprit, but your orders are above all and I will never go against them," Shalini said confidently.

Mr Rathi smiled and said, "Soon you will get visa and tickets along with a detailed plan. And remember, no public violence there; it could create problems in Malaysia. It would be a secret operation. One of our officers will accompany you. Start preparing."

"Yes sir," said Shalini.

And the video call was disconnected.

Arjun shut the laptop and put inside the bag. "Thank you sir!" Shalini said from behind.

Arjun moved his head back, "For what?"

"You recommended my name for Malaysia," she said with a little smile on her face.

Arjun finally zipped up his bag, put his cell phone in the pocket and turned to her. "Shalini! You have a strong motive behind joining IB, and I understand that," he started in a soft tone. "You are carrying a volcano of revenge within you. When a volcano erupts, it burns everything on its way. And the eruption of your revenge has already begun. I believe it will burn every odd thing on its way. You will leave no stone unturned in Pushkar's case.

"Shalini, your prey would be in front of you. Weave some kind of web around him that he is forced to come to India. There, take your revenge. None of the officers is better than you for this work," Arjun tapped Shalini's shoulder with a smile before leaving.

Where there's a will, there's a way

Mr Deepak Rathi with Mahesh Chandra, the head of RAW, had a meeting with the Home Minister in his office.

"Sir, the whole operation sketch is in front of you; we need your approval for its accomplishment," said Mr Chandra to the Home Minister.

The Home Minister listened and asked, "Guru Rajan or Shakeel are alleged for printing and supply of fake currency in India, and also they have been supplying arms and explosives in the country. They have indulged in threatening and killing people. Why have they have not been caught till now?"

"Sir, its unfortunate but it's true; they possess a massive internal network inside our country. Their information channels are spread throughout our police system to ministers and film industry. Before police could take any action against them, their channel cautioned them in advance and we missed them," said Mr Chandra

He continued ahead, "Fifteen years back, IB had accurate information of Guru Rajan being in Karachi. A team of four assassins was provided extensive training in the use of sophisticated arms and explosives and also briefed about the geography of the area.

"It was a zero-failure plan in place. But then the central government asked that the plan be put on hold. It was a disappointment. Why was the final approval not given to us? Guru Rajan would have definitely been eliminated."

"Hmm," the Home Minister got thoughtful for a moment after listening to all the points. He stood up from his chair and started walking in the room. Mr Rathi and Mr Chandra looked at each other. They were sitting patiently and waiting for his decision.

Finally, the Minister was back to his chair. "My approval is with you. Go ahead! Whatever support is needed, our department will do it. Abu Dhabi government will be taken into our confidence. But remember, no casualty of civilians in this operation," he said.

Shalini left for Malaysia and got a job in Four Seasons Resort as a room attendant with the name 'Monica'. Vijender Tyagi, an IB officer also joined her in the resort. He settled himself in the security and safety department of the resort.

In Abu Dhabi, Arjun had the complete layout of the place where Guru Rajan was living. The squad of four commandos joined him in Abu Dhabi. Now the squad had seven commandos in total. The operation plan was ready.

They chose midnight for the attack, it for two reasons – first, the area would be free from local citizen and second, Guru Rajan's henchmen would be unprepared for an attack on them.

The fully equipped commandos surrounded all the exit points of the place. Arjun with Govind reached the terrace. Two commandos entered from the main entrance, and the shootout began. One commando was controlling the backyard, and the other two entered from the southern entrance.

The sudden shootout startled the entire gang inside. They reached for their guns and explosives, nimbly. A rigorous shootout started from both the sides. Guru Rajan ran towards the stairs to reach the upper floor which led to the terrace. Arjun and Govind were already there.

Guru Rajan reached the upper floor and saw two commandos, guns in hand. He tried to shoot at them, but before he could press the trigger, a bullet hit his forehead from Arjun's gun. His body fell and rolled down from the stairs. That was the end of India's most wanted gangster. Further, the shootout continued for some time until each and every gang man was gunned down.

Shalini had her eye on every checked-in guest. According to Sunny Baweja, Pushkar was coming that day itself. But there was no sign of him anywhere. Somehow she managed to check the guest list of the day, but Pushkar's name was not there.

She went to Vijender, "Pushkar's name is not in the checked-in list," she said.

"I think he has changed his plan. I have been sitting in front of the computer screen for the whole day, I didn't see him either," said Vijender.

Later in the night, she informed Mr Rathi about there being no sign of Pushkar Mehta in the resort.

Next morning, Shalini was on duty at the pool side. She was placing fresh towels and robes on the pool chairs, when she heard a familiar husky voice, ordering a whisky on the pool side bar. She recognised the peculiar voice of Pushkar Mehta. She looked at the direction of the voice. The man was wearing sunglasses and was looking different. He had shoulder length hair, was clean shaved and there was a scar on the left side of his face. As she remembered, Pushkar used to keep a thick moustache; his hair was short and also had no scar on his face. The man's complexion was also fairer than Pushkar's.

To have a better look of him, she went near the bar. She noticed his body type, which was more or less like Pushkar. Then she came in front of him and greeted him warmly, "Good morning sir!"

The man looked at her casually and nodded his head in response. Till then, the bar staff had given him his drink and asked to sign on a paper. The man removed his sunglasses and signed the paper. That's the time Shalini looked at his eyes. She had seen the same eyes earlier also; it was Pushkar Mehta.

After he left, she checked the paper and noted his room number in her mind.

Later, she checked the name of the guest staying in that room number. The name mentioned was Nadeem Abraham. He came in disguise. She found his check-out date marked for the twentieth. So she had two days to fetch out information from him about Shakeel. And she could not forget her revenge; he had to pay her back for Gourav's murder.

Shalini met Vijender and told him about Pushkar. Vijender got surprised for a moment, "Oh! That's why we couldn't recognise him. Good job Shalini, must say." Further he continued, "Now we need to track everything about Pushkar. When he goes out? What he does all day? When is he alone? How does he like to spend his evenings?"

He gave her a spy earpiece for further secret communication between them. And also gave her micro cameras, which she had to fix in Pushkar's room. That could help in tracking his activities inside the room.

After spending an hour near the pool, Pushkar went into his room. He ordered his breakfast in the room only. And after that he put 'DND' on the door. He was inside his room for six hours and didn't come out. Around 3 o'clock, a person went into his room. Pushkar and the man had lunch together in the room. Around 5 o'clock that person came out. After half an hour, Pushkar also came out and went out of the hotel. Vijender and Shalini were waiting for that only. Shalini entered the room for cleaning. She had three micro audio-visual cameras. She quickly fixed the cameras on some unnoticeable places. Vijender was ready with his set up in a different location; he was instructing her over the spy microphone about the correct camera angle to cover the entire room.

"Good job Shalini, now Pushkar can be seen and heard also…" Vijender paused for a second, and quickly said, "Shalini, get out of the room, Pushkar has returned." Pushkar returned in fifteen minutes. This time he came along with four persons. Two of them walked down along with Pushkar to his room, and the other two were busy with some formalities on the reception counter.

Shalini joined Vijender at his location and quickly bumped the question as she got in, "Is he in?"

"Yes, he is, with two more people in the room," Vijender said without shifting his eyes from the laptop. He put the earphone on to hear their conversations, and said, "Only two cameras are working, it seems something has blocked the third camera."

Pushkar was clearly seen, he was sitting in the front of one of the cameras. Among two people, one had his back towards the camera, so his face was not visible, and the other person was partially seen.

Their conversation concluded that they were meeting some business tycoons the very next day and doing investments in their projects.

Pushkar called up someone and confirmed the timings of the meeting. He asked them to come to the hotel itself.

After disconnecting the phone line, he showed some photographs to the man whose face couldn't be seen. Pushkar was addressing the man as 'Bhai'.

"Who is this person?" Shalini muttered.

"Until they remove their belongings from the camera front, we can't see his face," said Vijender.

"Tomorrow they have a busy schedule, they have meetings lined up and in the evening they have a small party. And day after tomorrow Pushkar is leaving. So we have only tonight to interrogate him about Shakeel," Shalini added.

Vijender and Shalini were trying to focus on their conversation to fetch some more vital information out. And they learnt that Pushkar was leaving for Dubai in a private jet, along with the person he was addressing as bhai.

"Do as much planning you want to do, I will make you come back to India," Shalini muttered.

"How?" Vijender heard Shalini and asked.

Shalini showed him Pushkar's passport, which she had picked from his room. Vijender took that from her hand and looked at it. "It's a UAE passport of Nadeem Abraham, a forged one," he said. "He could manage another forged passport here also, and will escape easily," Vijender put his point.

"Yes, he could. But we will not spare him this time. He doesn't even know that his passport is missing; he is busy with meetings and all. Tomorrow morning anonymously we will inform the police that he has no passport with him. The police will arrest him and his nationality would be checked. UAE embassy will also go through Nadeem Abraham's authenticity of claiming his citizenship. And in the meantime, the Indian embassy will identify him as Pushkar and ask for his custody. When his identity would be disclosed, he would be arrested and sent back to India," Shalini narrated the whole consequences.

"Great! So you planned everything?" Vijender said flabbergasted.

Shalini gave a simple smile and focused back to Pushkar's room.

After an hour, their meeting got over. The man, who could partially be seen, stood up and went to the washroom. When he came out, he pulled up his jacket, which was kept on the table. As he pulled up the jacket, the camera captured the scene, and simultaneously a window flashed over the laptop screen. Now they could see the third person's face very clearly, he was sitting exactly in front of the hidden camera.

"Sha...keel... Ahmad!" Shalini and Vijender uttered simultaneously, in shock.

Vijender couldn't believe his eyes, "Is he really Shakeel?"

"Pushkar is addressing him as bhai, you heard, didn'tyou? And I have seen him before, he is Shakeel only," Shalini tried to clear the doubts.

"So, now, there is no meaning of interrogating Pushkar," said Vijender. "We should immediately inform Mr Rathi about this."

They called up Mr Rathi and informed him about Pushkar and Shakeel.

"What? Shakeel!" Mr Rathi uttered in amazement.

"Yes sir, Pushkar came in disguise to meet him. Together they are involved in some business project here. Tomorrow they are meeting some businessmen, and in the evening there is a party organised for them, and day after tomorrow, Pushkar and Shakeel are flying to Dubai in a private jet," said Shalini.

"I see," said Mr Rathi.

"Sir, this is the time we should plan something concrete. We can't let it go," said Shalini.

"Hmm, you both keep your eyes on them, I will get back to you soon with the plan," said Rathi and disconnected the phone call.

Mr Rathi immediately called up an emergency meeting of Joint Secretaries and Technical Department.

They worked out for long before coming to the plan. They analysed information, the risk, possible failure or success, and finally decided to execute it.

The Prime Minister was taken into confidence. He showed a green signal to the execution.

And any help from Indian Air Force was assured.

Shalini and Vijender were providing every bit of information of Shakeel to RAW.

Shakeel along with Pushkar and two more associates reached Langkawi International airport. Shalini and Vijender followed them to the airport, bought tickets for Hyderabad and got inside. They saw a flight attendant had accompanied the two men, and together they were proceeding to board the private flight.

Vijender communicated the take off time to the RAW.

In India, Indian Air Force jets were all set and waiting for orders from Air Traffic Control. The mission was to escort Shakeel's private jet once it entered Indian airspace and force it to land in Hyderabad.

After three hours and twenty minutes, they received information from ATC that the private jet has entered Indian airspace.

According to the plan, Indian jets escorted the private jet of Shakeel Ahmad and Pushkar Mehta. One of the Indian jets approached the private plane from below and to the left so that, the captainof the plane could easily see him.

The captain saw an Indian Air Force jet waggling his wings. That signalled the demand of the forced landing. He informed the passengers about an emergency landing in Hyderabad.

The announcement startled everyone in the plane. Pushkar went inside the pilot's cabin to know the matter and he learnt that it was a forced landing. He could see Indian Air Force jets around. He rushed to Shakeel nervously, "Bhai we are trapped."

Shakeel saw Indian jets around. He went to the cockpit and ordered the pilot to not land in India.

"Sir, I am sorry. I can't do this. It would be violation. It is an act of becoming suspicious. The Indian Air Force could even knock down the plane, if it doesn't land," the captain said.

Shakeel and Pushkar couldn't understand how to avoid the situation; they had not felt so helpless ever before.

Finally, the private plane was made to land in Hyderabad. Police was available on the spot to take into custody India's most wanted gangster. Shakeel, Pushkar and the other two associates were arrested.

Celebration was in the air. The head of RAW Mr Mahesh Chandra threw a party at his residence to celebrate the victory over two most wanted criminals of the country.

Mr Chandra raised his drink up and said, "Finally, the game of hide and seek came to an end. We knocked down Guru Rajan in Abu Dhabi and Shakeel will celebrate each night in jail. The court has given him life imprisonment. It's a remarkable success of our department on the ground of zero causality. A huge cheer for the team."

"CHEERS…" all said in chorus and raised their glasses in air.

"I would like to mention one of our officer's names, who has played an important role in the mission. Without her, it was not going to be that easy. She had joined just a few months back and it was her first mission. Shalini, you are incredible. Mr Rathi has told me everything about you," said Mr Chandra.

Everyone present cheered and clapped for her.

Shalini smiled and thanked him and the rest of the team for the appreciation.

When other officers were enjoying the music and drinks, Arjun came near Shalini.

"Congratulations," he whispered in her ear. Shalini turned around; Arjun was behind her with his glass in hand.

"Thank you," she said. "Congratulations to you too… Mission Abu Dhabi was well executed," she said.

"Thank you," said Arjun. He continued ahead, "Well, you don't seem satisfied with the success."

"Oh! Is it? Nothing like that, I am happy. This is what we wanted at the end," Shalini tried to smile and said.

"If you are happy, then why is your smile and your happiness not reaching your eyes?" Arjun asked looking into her eyes.

Shalini looked at Arjun, 'Can he read my face?' she thought.

Arjun continued, "Do you remember, I told you that day that you are the right person for the mission, and no one can replace you?" Shalini was looking at him spellbound. "And see you proved yourself. Today Shakeel Ahmad is in jail for life. And, Pushkar Mehta, he was sentenced to jail for seven years," said Arjun.

With the last sentence, Arjun noticed a change of facial expression in Shalini. Her eyes turned dry, few, thin wrinkles appeared between her eyebrows, and the fake smile on her face was about to fade in a moment.

Arjun didn't take his eyes off hers, he continued, "But Pushkar deserves more for his acts. See, mere seven years in jail can't give you a simple smile, how come it will give nation the peace?"

"Your revenge is still incomplete, right?" He directly asked Shalini.

Shalini thought for a second and said, "Sir, you are right. My revenge is his death. Gourav is dead because of him. He shouldn't be alive. But, he is imprisoned now and I am feeling helpless."

"If I give you a chance for your revenge, then?"

"You will give me the chance? How?" Shalini was bewildered.

"Pushkar has to be taken to another jail in a few days. This would be the time when you could change the game."

"Why are you helping me out in this?" She asked.

"Shalini, someone has to do it. People like him are of no use to the society. After seven years, he will be free and again he will indulge in his illegal business. And why seven years? He could use his source and power and manage to bail out in some time. He is a mere termite for the society and nothing else. Again our intelligence would be wasting its time finding him.

"If not you, then anyone among us could take charge of this. But, I well understand your mind. It is a duty for us, but, for you it is your revenge. Pushkar should only be your prey."

Arjun's words seemed most satisfying and desirable in the world to Shalini. That's what she wanted. How well Arjun understood her. She gazed at him mesmerised. Arjun blinked his eyes and nodded. "Come to bureau tomorrow, we'll discuss the execution plan. Hope you are in?" asked Arjun.

"Sure, I'm game," she smiled and said.

"Cheers!" Arjun chuckled his glass with Shalini's.

Behind the bars, Pushkar was sitting on his cot restlessly. His anxiety was palpable. He stood up and started moving from one end to another. 'Seven years of jail! How could it be possible? I can't spend even a single night here, no... no... no... I am Pushkar Mehta, I have money, and I have power. No one can detain me for long. My resources must be doing something to get me out of here...'

"You have some visitor," the guard said to Pushkar and unlocked the gate. Pushkar followed the attendant to the meeting area.

Pushkar saw a lady sitting over there in a pink shirt and black trousers. Her face was a little familiar, but still he was unable to recognise her.

"Yes," Pushkar uttered in a peculiar manner.

"Hello sir! How are you?" asked the lady with a smile. Suddenly she realised her mistake, looking at Pushkar's stern gesture and corrected herself, "Sorry, I just asked generally. How could anyone feel good in such a place? You would also be thinking about getting out from here as soon as possible, isn't it?" she said.

"Who are you?"

"Sunny has sent me here," she said in a very low voice.

"Sunny!" Pushkar was confused.

"Tomorrow you will be shifted to another jail, avail the chance to escape from."

"How?"

"The police van carrying you would be stopped just before the narrow bridge by a herd of goats. The driver and the other policemen would get down from the van and would look for the goatherd or get busy with dispersal of the goats. That time a sleeping gas capsule would be shot inside the van. You have to be very careful and save yourself from the gas; don't forget to keep a hankie over your nose and mouth. And keep this pin; you can open your shackle with it. Get the keys of the van's door and run towards the opposite side of the bridge. A black SUV would be waiting for you there."

Pushkar's eyes shone with the plan. He took the pin from her and asked, "Who are you? How does Sunny…" He got interrupted in between by the jail attendant, "Time's up, meeting time over. Let's go back."

"You will get all of your answer, wait till the right time comes," she said.

The police van was ready to take Pushkar to another location. His hands were shackled. Four policemen were accompanying him in the rear part of the van. One of them had locked the gate from inside and put the keys in his pocket.

Pushkar was sitting very calmly, waiting for the right time.

After twenty kilometres the van stopped. Ahead on a small bridge were a number of goats, blocking the way. The driver honked continuously, but in vain, the goats didn't give the van free way. Finally the driver got down and also the policeman sitting in the front. They looked for the goatherd, but no one was there. They started chasing them off.

Pushkar comprehended the situation; he pretended coughing and put his hankie over his mouth. Suddenly a bullet entered the van and that got filled with gas. Pushkar waited till the moment everyone fainted inside. He used the pin to open his shackle; it opened after a little effort. He quickly pulled out the door key from the police man's pocket and opened the door.

The smell of freedom brought a grin over his face. He ran madly in the opposite direction. After some distance, he could see a black SUV on the other side of the road. 'That's the vehicle for me,' he thought and ran towards that. He was waving and running towards the car.

The car sped towards Pushkar. Pushkar saw the car was coming to pick him up, so he stopped in the middle of the road and started panting. The car was coming closer to him but instead of slowing down, it accelerated. Pushkar signalled to stop, but the car had been accelerated enough to stop at the moment, and hit Pushkar. Pushkar's body flew in the air and dropped after a distance of nearly fifty meters.

In the state of semiconsciousness, Pushkar saw the lady in the pink shirt and black trousers. Pushkar had got several injuries; he was lying in a pool of blood. Somehow he managed to utter when she came closer, "Why did you do this to me? Who are you?"

She bent a little and said venomously, "I had to do it. You deserve it. Hope you remember Gourav Mishra, whom you rubbed out very easily. I'm his wife, Shalini. Today my revenge has been completed." Pushkar's gaze had been on her face, until his last breath.

Shalini sat on the road and cried all her heart.

Suddenly she felt a hand over her shoulder. "Are you okay?" Arjun asked. "He is dead." Then he turned to Shalini, saw her red swollen eyes. She was looking tired and vulnerable. He slowly pulled her towards himself and hugged her. "Relax; it's the end of your mournful life. Close this chapter for ever. Nothing is perpetual in life, not even your tears. Tomorrow is a new day, a new hope, a new challenge, go with it. Allow your life a new, fresh smile which motivates not only you, but others also."

Shalini didn't remember when she had felt such relaxation and peace in the last few years, which she was feeling right then in Arjun's arms. Every time, his words did some magic on her.

Breaking news!

Pushkar Mehta came under the wheels of a speeding car while escaping from the police custody.

The alleged of various conspiracies, Pushkar Mehta tried to flee from the police van, which was taking him to another jail. He was running on the adjacent road when he was hit by a speeding car. It was a severe accident; he died on the spot.

★★★